WHITEOUT

D0302193

GABRIEL DYLAN

RED EYE

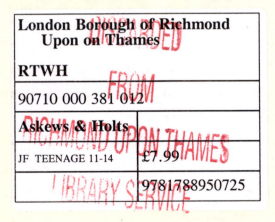

Chapter One

If it all went wrong, reckoned Charlie, at least it would be over quickly.

He crunched to a halt where the slope fell away into nothingness, and carefully laid his snowboard on top of the deep drifts at his feet. A wave of panic washed over him as he stared down at the tiny streets and buildings that nestled in the valley miles below, just visible through a veil of wispy cloud. He wrenched his eyes away, sank into the snow, and started to slide his feet into the decrepit bindings. The Santa Cruz board was battered and chipped, the edges dull and worn. Where a blue-cloaked skeleton had once grinned manically out from the topsheet, now a myriad of scratches and scuffs made the image almost impossible to make out.

Charlie clicked the last strap into place, tightened the bindings, and reached up to pause the Biffy Clyro track that blared through his headphones.

The sudden silence made his head reel for a moment and he took a frigid, calming breath then leaned back and felt the snow mould around him.

He'd pictured the view countless times over the past six months but, even so, it was far more spectacular than he'd imagined. It had taken him most of the afternoon to hike across from one side of the peak to the other, but the effort had been more than worth it.

Away from the tiny resort they were staying in, there really was nothing but empty wilderness. The south side of the mountain stretched down at his feet, a pristine fun-park of untouched, flawless snow, and across from him – all around him – lay nothing but distant rocky peaks and vast, deserted forests.

And there was nobody there to enjoy the view but him.

They'd been warned not to go off-piste. The instructors were particularly frantic about that rule and the consequences of breaking it.

Avalanches. Death. Rocks. Death. Freezing. Death.

Take your pick.

But Charlie was pretty sure that he didn't care either way.

Even with the deserted splendour of the Austrian Alps laid out before him, he couldn't help but dwell on the fact that soon he would be slammed back into reality.

Four more days.

And at least three of those were likely to be ruined by the huge winter storm that was currently sweeping in his direction.

Charlie swore and looked down at the drop just a few feet from where his board nestled among the snow. Now that he sat there, actually looking down at the mountain he had planned to ride, he wasn't really sure it was doable. His heart was hammering in his chest as if he'd just run a marathon, and he knew it wasn't just the exertion from the hike that was causing it.

From nowhere, a tiny voice started to chatter away at the back of his head.

Maybe nobody tackled the south side for a reason.

Maybe the instructors had been right.

Maybe he might not walk away from this.

Charlie chewed his bottom lip, his confidence

wavering. But there really was nothing waiting for him back home, was there? Nothing but misery, and it wasn't going to get better any time soon.

He nodded to himself and stood up on his snowboard, hopping from tip to tip to try to warm up, feeling the snow under his feet crunch satisfyingly. He stole another quick glance at the powder field below him, imagined himself flying down the vertiginous slope, catching an edge, hitting a rock, breaking his leg, then lying out until dark and beyond – the barren, starless night slowly sapping the life out of him.

Charlie took another snort of Alpine air. He *could* turn and walk away. He *could* trudge back over the mountaintop and take the reds and blues back down to the village. He knew the risks. The same way he knew that if it didn't work out, nobody was going to miss him anyway.

Screw it.

Before he had time to change his mind, he lined up the nose of the board with the drop below and leaned his weight forwards so that he started to slip down the slope. Just as the board gained momentum and reached the point of no return, Charlie could have sworn he heard a voice behind him, words calling on the wind. But by then it was too late to do anything but look forwards, bend his knees and let gravity do the rest.

Then he was away.

For what felt like an eternity he freefell down the mountain, the wind in his ears, his heart pounding, the world a vertical blur. An instant before his board could slip out of control he dug in his heels and carved a steep, banking turn through the snow. A quick shift to the right, and he darted the other way, his snowboard chattering underneath his feet. Snow sprayed around him like a cloud of vapour, biting at the exposed skin on his face.

Each time he felt himself getting too much speed, Charlie dug in his heels or his toes and felt the pace die away for an instant. Then he tore off again, only faintly aware that he was shouting – a long, high cry of excitement tearing from his lungs. The speed of his run transformed the frozen wilderness around him into an indistinct kaleidoscope of whites and greys, his mind focused on nothing more than the bite of his snowboard, the winding dance of the mountain.

It was on his sixth or seventh turn that he noticed the low rumble, like thunder across the valley. Without slowing, he slipped on to his toe edge, reached out low with his fingertips towards the snow to steady himself and chanced a look back up to where he had come from.

A horizon of jumbling chaos loomed above him. Tumbling downwards was a wave of rock and snow, the grey sky gone, a cloud of debris and ice filling the air. Charlie tasted bile at the back of his throat.

The heartbeat that he took his sight off the slope was all it needed for him to lose his concentration. His board caught an edge, and he slipped backwards and slammed his head on the snow. His goggles were torn away from his eyes, his legs above his head, all sense of direction gone.

Charlie didn't have time to be scared.

As he flew down the slope on his back, a deep, booming rumble shuddered around him, through him, growing closer all the time. He managed to slam his legs down into the snow, felt the edge of his board bite. The blur around him slowed, and as he had time to process what was happening he registered the snow that had found its way under his shirt, down his pants, into his mouth. He dragged to a halt then scrabbled to his knees, fighting to suck a whisper of air into his lungs.

The roaring was everywhere now, in his head, his chest, running through his body like a current. He turned to his right, saw the vast wave of snow that was a heartbeat from sweeping him away ... and then everything went black.

Chapter Two

Nico heard the sound just as he arrived back in the village, still absorbing the fact that, against all the odds, he'd survived another day with no broken bones. A rumble, deep and powerful, like the anger of a distant earthquake, cracked across the range.

Nico felt a shiver of panic running down his back, then he caught Stefan's eye and noticed the lack of concern there.

"Was that thunder?" asked one of the students, a good-looking girl that Nico was fairly sure was called Leandra. He didn't know much about her, other than that they shared an art class and he'd seen her paintings displayed in the school reception. He'd never actually been brave enough to speak to her, but he'd seen her a few times in the library, and had peered up from the safety of his computer screen to listen in on her conversations.

Leandra's thick black hair was stuffed under

a clunky orange helmet, and her large, dark eyes shone out anxiously from under its chipped rim.

Stefan shook his head. "No. That's an avalanche. But it's over there, up on the other side of the mountain, off-piste. No one skis up there. So I don't think we need to worry."

As the eyes of several of the students in his group widened, Nico wondered if his relief at the day's survival had been somewhat premature, but Stefan smiled playfully.

"We get lots of avalanches in the winter. Sometimes we set them off ourselves with dynamite, just to make it safer on the lower pistes. With the dump of snow that they're expecting to fall over the next few days, I think we might be hearing that sound a little more."

One of the boys, Ryan, turned in Stefan's direction. He was tall, well over six foot, and built like a bull – the kind of kid that Nico wished he could be reincarnated as. Back at home, Ryan was captain of the rugby team, king of the common room and a minor celebrity among a sea of sixth formers. But while he could have easily acted like a dick, he didn't – even towards nerds like Nico. Since they'd arrived in Austria, he'd been polite, respectful and eager to listen to all Stefan's instructions.

Plus he was a natural athlete. Much to Nico's jealousy, he'd picked up skiing in just a few days and was already far ahead of the rest of the group.

"You think we'll be able to ski tomorrow? You think this storm will be as bad as they're saying?"

Stefan shrugged in response. "They always exaggerate it in this part of the Alps, but it does look pretty bad. If the reports turn out to be right, I doubt we'll be able to set foot out of the front door tomorrow. If there's as much snow as they say, we won't even be able to open it."

As if in acknowledgement of the instructor's words, Nico noticed that a slow trickle of flakes had started to fall from the sky. He looked upwards and saw that the thin grey clouds had given way to a much more menacing, bruised gloom.

Ryan flicked at the flakes that settled in his fringe and pulled his beanie down an inch lower. "Here it comes, then. You sure we can't have one more run before we go in, Stefan?"

"No. That's it for today, I'm afraid. We'll get some food in us, get the fires going. It'll be – what do you English say? – Cosy? Is that the word?" The ski instructor nodded to himself, then started to lead the party of students back through Kaldgellan towards its lone hotel.

It was growing darker by the minute, a combination of falling dusk and an ominous sky. Every other day this week, there had been streetlights and lanterns glowing all the way back from the lift station to the hotel, and Christmas lights twinkling in the windows of the handful of shops.

But tonight the track back from the slopes was unusually dark; wooden shutters closed and candles unlit.

As they reached the village centre, Nico picked up on an air of bustle among the few people on the street. He recognized a couple of the locals he'd seen earlier that week packing up their sleds to hike over to the main lift station, presumably getting down the mountain before the storm came in. Nico had spent the day shivering so much he could barely concentrate, but even so he'd heard about the impending snowfall and its ramifications for the rest of the trip.

Nico jumped at a loud rattle as the shutter slid

down on the village's lone café. Stefan spotted the owner – a chubby, friendly local man in his fifties – hovering just outside the darkened building. He was squinting down at his watch, and the instructor held up his hand to pause Nico's group.

"Ho, Marlon, what's with all the closing? Where's everyone going to?"

The owner had a harassed shine in his bloodshot eyes, and he shook his head. "Just getting away before this storm comes in, is all. I don't want to be stuck up here for three days with no way of getting down. They're saying that the winds will get so bad they'll shut the cable cars down. I don't want to be trapped up here like a prisoner, no thank you."

Nico felt a nervous twinge in his gut, but Stefan grinned at the owner. "What about the money you could make? There must be nearly thirty students staying at the hotel. Think of the cakes and cappuccino they're going to need!"

Marlon didn't reply or even crack a smile. Nico watched as he turned away and continued to quickly stuff his belongings into the back of his battered wooden sled. Stefan shrugged and turned back to his group.

"What will we do all day tomorrow if we can't ski?"

Nico looked at the speaker, a tall, skinny girl called Ellie. He'd gone to primary school with her, watched her try to cope with her parents' messy divorce, danced with her at the year seven disco … only to somehow lose touch with her as they crept into adulthood.

Stefan smiled in Ellie's direction. "I'm sure you'll think of something. Worse case scenario you can sneak out and build a snowman. Me, I plan to sleep. I'm back to university next month for my finals and tomorrow might be my last chance for a guilt-free day in bed."

Ellie's blue eyes were locked on to Stefan, a glint of admiration hovering there that gave Nico a twinge of envy. She was pretty, although he wondered if she'd be even more attractive without so much make-up. Her thick woollen hood obscured most of her features, but in the half-light Nico could make out skin that had been coated with a more than liberal helping of fake tan, flanked by a pair of hoop earrings that nestled in the curls of her long, bleached hair.

"I want to get to university and do fashion, down in London. But first I've got to get through my A-levels. My parents say it'll never happen, that people from our part of the city don't belong at uni. And if I don't get at least Cs in my mocks, they say they're going to make me leave and get a job. I just hope I prove them wrong."

Stefan flashed his winning smile. "You'll do it. Just believe in yourself."

Nico turned as a figure surged out of the gloom, and watched Stefan wave a gloved hand in its direction.

"Hey, Matthias, you not staying for a drink tonight?"

There were four ski instructors that worked for the hotel in Kaldgellan, but Matthias was the oldest by quite some way. Nico had heard Stefan telling one of the other students that Matthias had lived in the village all his life and had never strayed far from the isolated resort.

Normally Matthias and the other instructors stayed in the hotel bar after dark, swapping stories and ridiculing the awful skiing of some of their guests, which Nico was sure included him. But now the older man shook his head slowly.

"No, I ... I can't stay. It's a ... a family thing. I need to get down to the valley, and if I don't go tonight..."

Matthias had his skis over one shoulder and seemed about to say something. Then he shook his head and looked up at the snow that was steadily falling from above. He didn't speak for a moment, and in the half-light it looked to Nico as if he were shaking.

One of Matthias's big, gloved hands swept out and clapped Stefan on the shoulder. "My group are inside, getting warm. You should take this lot in. You're a great guy, Stefan. Look after yourself, the next few days. Have a drink for me tonight, eh?"

Matthias was a gruff, bearded Austrian, the kind of man that looked to Nico as if he could wrestle a bear − but there was something odd on his face, something that Nico found unnerving. Stefan seemed to pick up on it too, and he took a step closer to the older man.

"Hey, whatever's wrong, I'm sure it'll work itself

out. You want me to stay for a while, talk things through?"

Matthias shook his head and slid his bulky hand off Stefan's shoulder. While Nico watched the conversation unfold, the rest of his group chatted and milled around, staring up at the descending flakes that grew heavier by the second. They'd been in the Alps for three days and although there had been showers, this was the first real snowfall since they'd arrived.

Matthias leaned closer to Stefan. "No. Just need to get down the mountain. You look after yourself and this lot. Be lucky, if you can. I need to get over to the lift before this wind gets any worse. It's come in a lot earlier than they said it would."

He strode off in the direction of his car, an old Jeep with snow chains shining on the tyres. Without a backwards glance he jumped in, slammed the door, revved the engine then skidded away through the snow. Stefan watched him go, a look of confusion on his face.

"You OK, Stefan?"

The instructor nodded vaguely, tracking Matthias's tail lights as they flickered towards the lift station. Stefan's eyes fell on Nico, trying and failing to hide a glimmer of exasperation. The instructor had warned him about the cold that morning, but even so Nico had come out on to the slopes with nothing but a long-sleeved top with a *Walking Dead* T-shirt over it and, as Stefan had predicted, he'd spent the day shivering.

"Yeah, I'm fine. But you look a little frozen."

Stefan shook his head and gestured towards the Panoramic Hotel, a faded, dumpy, three-storey building a few metres away. "Come on, you guys, nearly there. Let's get inside before this snow *really* starts to fall."

Chapter Three

Charlie was stuck in a dream.

He was somewhere back in time – a year ago, maybe more, in one of his worst memories. The twisted faces of those around him were only a heartbeat from morphing into something much more monstrous.

He and a social worker sat in the headmaster's tiny office, the news getting worse and worse. A hail of words stuttered out of the teacher's mouth like gunfire.

Fading light. Building swell. Little hope. Halting the search.

Charlie wanted more than anything to be away from this place, this memory.

Then he was.

Pain started to cut through his dream, vague at first, then more severe. There was a tightness around his throat like a noose. It wasn't just sadness that choked him, but something physical, biting into his neck below his Adam's apple. The sound of his own gagging started to wake him and he became aware that he was being pulled backwards, into the light, someone or something roughly dragging him by his collar.

He opened his eyes and it all came back to him. The blindingly fast powder run, the rumble from above, the huge wave of snow and debris that picked him up and swept him along like a piece of stray driftwood. He coughed, spat out a mouthful of snow and took a deep breath. He realized that he had been gasping for air, starving for it.

Rolling on to his knees, he stared back up the way he had come and saw a landscape a world away from the one he had admired just moments ago. Where there had been flawless, pristine blankets of fresh snow there was now a sprawling chaotic mass, as if the entire mountainside had been unearthed and churned up by huge, unseen diggers. Here and there, chunks of grey rock protruded through the snow like mines and Charlie realized how lucky he was to be in one piece.

He coughed, spat, staggered to his feet through a

mist of dancing stars and suddenly remembered that he wasn't alone.

A few feet away from him, a figure watched him through a pair of mirrored ski goggles. There was a snowmobile a little way behind them on the slope, and Charlie realized that the stranger must have seen him fall and set off to rescue him. The figure lifted a gloved hand to their face and pulled down the scarf that covered their mouth.

"What the hell were you thinking?"

His rescuer's face was covered by a hood and goggles, but her voice was unmistakably female and foreign. When she spoke, her English had a harsh, angular tone to it. And there was no mistaking the anger in her voice.

Charlie tried to speak but found that he couldn't get the words out. He coughed again, brushed the snow out of his hair and eyes and shook his head. "What?" he sputtered.

The girl lifted her goggles and stared at him, incredulous. "*Dummkopf*! Out here. On this slope. What were you thinking?"

Charlie spat at his feet. A mixture of ice and blood splattered on to the churned-up debris. His head was pounding, and he squinted against the snow that was steadily falling from above and turned to the girl wearily. "What's it to you?"

The girl's grey eyes blazed and she lashed out, catching Charlie full on the side of his face with her fist. He staggered backwards and struggled to stay on his feet. The girl poked a threatening finger in his direction.

"I had to come down here and save you from choking, that's what! *Scheisse*, you don't deserve to be alive! You idiots, coming out here, thinking you're something cool. What if there'd had been skiers below you, or hikers? What if you'd brought the mountain down on top of them?"

The girl was beyond furious and Charlie took another step away from her. He realized he was still strapped into his snowboard by one foot, and clumsily bent down and unclipped it. The other binding had snapped off and must have been buried in the snow somewhere alongside his goggles, gloves and headphones, probably lost forever. He gingerly stood back up and sighed.

"I knew it was just me out here. I wouldn't put anyone else in danger. And I'm sorry you had to come and dig me out."

The girl looked down at his snowboard and shook her head slowly. "That board must be twenty years old. From the nineties or something, a relic! You shouldn't be out here. Do you even know anything about the mountains? Have you ever set foot on snow before this week? Go back to your little group of English friends. The sooner you're gone the better!"

Charlie experienced a mixture of anger and guilt at what he'd done. His words came out before he had time to regulate them.

"I know the mountains and I can ride well enough. The board was my dad's, and yeah, it's old, but I can still use it better than anyone else I've seen on these mountains all week. I'm sorry you had to come down here, dig me out. I didn't want that to happen. But I go home in a few days and I wanted to see what else was out here."

The girl laughed, but there was no humour in the sound.

"Well, now you know, don't you? I hope you enjoyed your little run, the one that brought half the mountain down. You know this place is off limits.

People have died in these mountains. A l
People I cared about. I heard Stefan te
group on your first day here. *Nobody* com
unless they want to wind up under the ground."

Charlie nodded slowly. He felt tired and hollow,
horribly aware that his body was a mass of aches
and pains. He didn't want to argue. He just wanted
to go back to the Panoramic Hotel and lie down
somewhere.

"Look, I'm sorry, really, I didn't want to upset
anyone, or—"

The girl glared at him and stormed back up to her
snowmobile. Halfway there, she paused and turned
round. "Why did you do it, then? For the rush?
So you had a great story to boast to your friends
about?"

Charlie rubbed at the spot on his jaw where she
had punched him and shook his head. "I don't have
any friends. And even if I did, I wouldn't tell them
about this."

The girl snorted. "What, then? A death wish?"

Charlie held the girl's eyes for a moment, while
her words seemed to drill into his skull. He felt his
vision start to blur and he found himself wiping

at his eyes with the back of his hand. Instead of answering her he bent down, retrieved his broken board and started to trudge down through the snow. In places the drifts were waist-deep, and he struggled and slipped as he tried to put some distance between himself and the girl.

It was growing darker by the second. Far below, the orange lights of the village twinkled in the twilight. It was going to take Charlie hours to reach Kaldgellan and he suddenly realized the lunacy of his plan.

It was a few minutes before Charlie heard the noise of an engine starting and revving. Seconds later, the girl's snowmobile slid to a halt alongside him. He couldn't see her eyes. Instead his own dishevelled reflection peered back at him in the mirrored lenses, snow caked in his messy dark hair, something like regret swimming in his brown eyes.

When the girl spoke, her voice had lost its angry edge and her words were flat and emotionless.

"It's getting dark. And this storm is only going to get worse. If you try to make your way down the mountain and back across the valley chances are you're going to fall, trigger another slip or freeze to death. And I don't want any of those on my conscience."

She gestured to the seat behind her.

"So you better get on. And hope I'm not so pissed that I throw you off."

Chapter Four

From her seat on the sill of her second-floor bedroom window, Tara watched the light gradually drain out of the day. She moved closer to the frosted glass, nestling into her hoodie as she felt the draft hissing from the sides of the pane. If she squinted, she could just see a procession of laughing, chatting figures, making their way back from the lift station, skis and snowboards clutched under their arms. The sky that brooded above their heads was the colour of slate, stark white flecks of confetti whirling above them on the wind.

They better have enjoyed their time out on the slopes, mused Tara, because for the next few days they were going to be confined to the hotel. And Tara knew only too well how little fun that was.

The hot topic at breakfast that morning had been the storm that was due in. Tara had been listening to one of the instructors calling it a whiteout and explaining that once the blizzard arrived, any skiing and snowboarding was going to be officially cancelled for the day – the lifts shut down, the runs closed off. Tara had wanted to hear more, but just then Mrs Newman had thundered over and started rinsing her in front of the whole school party. And that was pretty much the last bit of contact with the outside world Tara had had.

She shook her head, checked her phone for what must have been the hundredth time in the last hour, and swore quietly.

Nothing. Not a thing.

There'd been no internet or signal since breakfast, and it was really starting to piss her off. She swore again, tossed her shiny iPhone back on the bed and was just about to go back to watching the progress of the tiny figures on their way back from the lift when there was an urgent knock on her bedroom door.

"Tara! Can you open up, please? I need to get changed and get down to dinner but I have to see you before they start serving."

Tara sighed, yawned, stumbled over to the door

and pulled it open a fraction. Mrs Newman's stern, pinched face peered at her through the sliver between door and frame. She had her padded purple North Face jacket zipped up to her chin, a pink snood just below her mouth. Flecks of melting snow glistened in her hair.

"I'll get you some food brought up here tonight, but I *do not* want you down there, mixing with the others. You're staying here, in your room, staring at the walls if you have to. You can do your psychology or sociology study if you're bored. But don't even think about leaving your room, or sticking so much as one foot into the snow outside. You understand?"

Tara shrugged. "It's so cold tonight I don't want to go out anyway, so I'm not really bothered."

She pushed a long strand of blond hair out of her eyes then glanced back at Mrs Newman with as much disdain as she could muster. The teacher's scowl deepened, the lines around her eyes and on her forehead becoming more pronounced.

"You might think this is all a joke, Tara. But let me assure you, if I find you on the boys' floor again after dark I'll take you down to the valley, throw you in a hire car and drive you to the airport myself, no matter how bad the weather gets."

Tara shrugged and looked down at her nails. When her family's money had run out and she'd been thrust into the horrors of comprehensive education, she never dreamed it would be this bad.

Mrs Newman pushed the door wider, her face flushed with agitation. "I don't care what you get up to at home but there are rules here. You might think you're untouchable but you're not. And roll your eyes at me again and you'll stay in your room until we fly home."

Mrs Newman waited for a response, but Tara knew she when she was cornered and she forced herself to bite back an acid retort. There was a long silence and then the teacher nodded with satisfaction and pushed the door to. Tara listened to her footsteps as she thumped down the stairs.

"Bitch," Tara muttered.

She turned and slinked back over to the bed to retrieve her phone. Thumbing on to Snapchat, she was met with the all-too-familiar *Cannot connect to server* message. Those four words had been the best it or any other app or website had to offer since just after breakfast. And no matter how many times

Tara obsessively checked, there was no change.

Pulling her fleeced hoodie tighter around her shoulders, Tara turned her attention back to the window and watched as the tiny figures trudged back through the storm towards the warm light of the hotel.

Chapter Five

Without the background drone of the television, the dining room seemed strangely sombre, Nico realized.

Even though most of the seats were occupied with babbling students and a raging fire filled one corner of the rustic room, there was still something missing without the battered old relic of a TV and the smaller screens dotted around the room.

There was supposed to be a football match on the television tonight, England versus Russia. Nico didn't even like football. He couldn't kick a ball to save his life unless he had an Xbox controller in his hand, but he liked the way that when a big game was on TV it brought everyone closer together. It made him feel a little bit more of a part of things.

But now the football was the latest casualty of the blizzard that shuddered and gasped outside, its exhalations seeming to almost flex the flimsy walls of the hotel back in on themselves. Nico had never heard a storm quite like it, but then he'd never been out of Bristol in pretty much his entire life so he didn't have a lot to compare it to.

Television wasn't the only casualty. The internet had gone too, not only on their phones and tablets, but also on the tired old computer in the lobby. Nico had gone on there earlier to try to send an email home to his mum but there was no connection. And there was zero signal on his phone.

So for now there was no *Minecraft*, no *Grand Theft*, no kind of online entertainment at all. He was so used to the students around him having glowing screens in their hands that their absence now seemed strangely unsettling. He peered over at his best friend Chris. "Nothing on yours either?"

Chris shook his head, scratched at his long greasy hair then went miserably back to the last of his supper. Nico watched him for a moment then leaned back in his chair and glanced around the room.

A host of glassy-eyed deer and foxes stared down at him from the spots on the woodchip walls where their unfortunate heads had been mounted. There were dozens of the creatures, their mouths forever frozen in a mask of redundant aggression and all-too-real surprise. There was even a huge black bearskin in one corner, suspended upside down so that its rear paws almost touched the ceiling. Nico noticed that several of the students had placed pieces of their evening meal – some blackened and burnt chicken nuggets – in its jaws, skewering the chunks on the dead bear's teeth. That's how bad the cooking was.

To be fair, the poor dinner wasn't really the fault of the two Polish girls who dashed from kitchen to servery to table, bringing out a succession of plates of overcooked chicken nuggets, greasy chips and brown, wilting lettuce. The hotel manager had gone home sick, Nico heard, and left the two waitresses in charge of pretty much the whole hotel. And they were probably only a few years older than the students they were cooking for.

But even before the food had come out there had been a bleak mood in the hotel that evening. Maybe it was the storm and the fact that there was unlikely to be any more skiing for the next few days. Maybe it was because the trip was going by a little too quickly. Or maybe it was the lack of glowing screens, the temporary disappearance of any contact with the outside world beyond the sleepy Austrian village.

Whatever it was, the sense of holiday celebration had vanished tonight.

Like Matthias, the other ski instructors who usually stood at the bar and drank beers and shots and hurled jokes at the students had also made other plans, leaving Stefan as their sole representative. He was chatting away to a striking but hard-faced girl at the bar. She had long black hair, shaved at the sides and pulled into a ponytail, and moody, piercing grey eyes. A silver ring in her nose shimmered in the dim light. She wore a pair of ski dungarees and a vest top. Nico studied her for a moment, making sure she wasn't looking in his vicinity. Her upper body was skinny, but she looked toned and athletic. Nico was fairly sure he had seen her out on the mountain a few days ago, leading a group of walkers off-piste. Whatever it was she was bending Stefan's ear about now, she didn't look happy at all.

As if they sensed Nico watching, the two of them abruptly broke off their conversation and stared over in his direction.

Nico felt his face burn red and he studied his

blank phone screen as fervently as he could. After a few seconds, he broke cover and realized that they weren't looking at him at all. Instead, their attention was focused on somebody else who had just walked into the dining room behind him.

Nico glanced around and saw Charlie push past the table, dark hair hanging down into his eyes. He was wearing a tatty hoodie and a pair of ripped jeans, and his eyes never left the floor as he walked towards the servery.

Now there, thought Nico, was somebody who didn't fit in anywhere. Charlie made Nico happy to be one of the geeks. It was as if there was a dark cloud permanently over the boy, and Nico noticed that none of the group even acknowledged him as he made his way across the room.

Charlie had appeared a few months ago, two weeks into term, just as A-level classes were underway. There was a lot of talk about him. Rumours bounced around that he had been thrown out of another school, had endured a horrific home life and had been mixed up with drugs, but Nico reckoned that nobody really knew the truth. The police had turned up at their school once or twice and Nico had seen Charlie being escorted to meet them. And from the look on his face it wasn't for a community service award. There was even a theory doing the rounds that his dad was in prison for murder. Nico didn't know if any of these stories were true, but they would explain why Charlie kept himself to himself and didn't mix with the other students.

Charlie studied art alongside Nico, but he'd never talked to anyone in that class either – he didn't seem to have any friends at all. Nico had been more than surprised to see him on the coach when they had left their school in Bristol. During the twenty-seven-hour journey to Austria, whenever Nico had looked in Charlie's direction, he had been either asleep or staring glassily out of the window with his headphones in.

It had been the first day on the snow, as they'd gathered to be divided into different ability groups, that Nico had heard Malachi, Jordan and some of the other sporty boys laughing and sniggering. At first he'd thought he was the source of their amusement. It wouldn't have been the first time.

But when he'd turned round he had seen Charlie

stumble out of the hotel into the snow. Under the arm of his parka he held a battered, stickered-up old snowboard that looked like it had been found gathering dust in somebody's loft. His gloves and trousers resembled clothing that had come from a second-hand store and his snowboard boots were partly held together with strips of silver duct tape. If Charlie had heard the sniggers he didn't show it.

But the laughing had stopped when, just to the side of the lift, Charlie buckled in and rose to his feet. He had leaned left and right as if stretching, jumped the board round and then zoomed away across the slope in a blur. As he went, he threw the board this way and that at will, letting loose a dazzling array of jumps and flips as he rode.

Quite where Charlie had learned how to snowboard like that was a mystery, just like Charlie himself. And it had certainly shut up the boys from the rugby team.

As if they'd read his mind, a cry went out from those assembled at the other end of the room, and Nico spun round to see Ryan and his group sitting around a table, playing that strange game where you try to throw a plastic bottle in the air and make it land again. It was a game Nico had never understood, but then he supposed he wasn't really sporty enough to ever be good at throwing balls, bottles or anything else for that matter.

Watching them, Nico wondered if the boys were part of a hive mind, like the Borg from *Star Trek*. When news had gone around that there was going to be a sixth-form ski trip, ten of the thirty places had been snatched up by the rugby team. They could have gotten more than a little bit rowdy, bored as they were, but Ryan seemed to keep them all in check. Or maybe it was Ryan's athletic female friend, Shiv, who had been accepted into the rugby inner circle in a way Nico never would, and who seemed to lend a little calm to the testosterone-fuelled gathering.

Even the thuggish blond-haired one, Jordan, whose dad was rumoured to be affiliated to some of the scarier gangs in Bristol, was much less offensive out here on the trip than he usually was back at sixth form. Underneath his curly hair he had a cruel, mean face and heavy-lidded, emotionless eyes. Back at home he seemed to spend the majority of his time slouching in the common room, grime music blasting out of his mobile phone.

Nico tried to avoid the common room, but on one of the few occasions when the IT suites were shut and he'd stumbled his way in there, Jordan had purposefully barged into him, sending him sprawling into a nearby table. The boy's cold, shark-like glare and scabbed knuckles had prompted Nico to very quickly apologize and move away.

Nico decided to look away before he was caught staring. Two tables of girls sat next to the rugby boys. While most of them leaned together, chatting or feverishly checking their phones, a few of them cast sad, longing looks at Ryan and the better-looking boys on the team. Nico knew some of the girls and had even spoken once or twice to a couple of them, but most of them ignored him or treated him as if he was some annoying little brother. One of them, Tara, was conspicuous by her absence, and Nico had heard a rumour that she'd been confined to her quarters for the day by Mrs Newman for some heinous crime, though he didn't know what.

"Two days of this, sitting here listening to that

lot cheer and shout, and I'll be dying to go home," mumbled Chris.

Nico nodded and Chris gestured out through the large bay window that ran along one side of the dining room.

"Look at all this snow. It's like Narnia out there. You think they'll let us out tomorrow?"

Nico shrugged. It sounded more and more as if the lifts would be shut, the resort closed and skiing pretty much off the table for the rest of the trip. He had spent his sixteen years coming to terms with the fact that he was rubbish at all sports, and he had discovered this week that skiing was no exception to that rule. All the same, he didn't want to be imprisoned inside for the rest of the trip with the rugby boys for company, or lose out on the few days' skiing he had left.

The teachers, hunched over their beer and wine around a small table in a far corner of the room, looked to be equally dejected. Mr Down seemed half-drunk, Mr Potter exhausted and Mrs Newman just her plain old miserable self. Maybe, Nico thought, they just wanted to go home.

A gasp went up as the wind shook the glass of

the windowpanes and the lights above their heads rattled and flickered. Nico glanced at his phone once again.

Nothing.

It was going to be a long night.

Chapter Six

It was one of the girls that found the blood.

Leandra hadn't been able to sleep, she told Charlie. First it had been the screeching wind that had stirred her. Later, in the dark hours past midnight, the creaks and groans of the old hotel had jerked her awake whenever she'd started to drift. Finally, as the first grey streaks of dawn had seeped in through the shutters of her dorm, she had given in and thrown back the covers.

The other girls in her room had still been snoring and twitching, exhausted from their time on the slopes, but Leandra had staggered up, thrown on a hoodie and wandered downstairs. She'd wanted to look outside, she said, to see if the snowfall was as spectacular as Stefan predicted it was going to be, to see if the drifts were really up to the top of the door. Her first destination had been the front of the lobby and the battered glass doors that opened out into the snow.

Her screams had woken Charlie in an instant. At first he thought he was at home, his gran moaning and crying out from the room next door. He had been down the flight of stairs to the lobby even before the last tendrils of dreams had fully gone and he'd realized where he was. Leandra had been standing there, sobbing, clinging on to the wall.

He knew her a little from two of the classes he was failing and she'd chatted to him once or twice, although he couldn't have said anything about her other than her name. But before he had been able to move she had her arms draped around him, her thick black hair pressed against the side of his face. All he was wearing was an old T-shirt and a pair of shorts, while Leandra didn't seem to have much more on than a hoodie. Charlie had found it hard not to feel uncomfortable as she mumbled what had happened. He'd put one arm around her while trying to work out what had made her scream.

Then he saw the blood.

It was as if somebody had stamped on a giant raspberry just outside the front door, in the knee-high snow, then dragged it away so that it left a long trail of juice and debris to signpost which way it had been taken. A few feet was all you could see before everything melted into the blizzard outside, snow hurrying this way and that like ash after a fire. But there was no mistaking that the trail was made of blood.

Lots of it.

Charlie used his one free hand to wipe at his bleary eyes and shuffled across towards the door, Leandra still pressed against him. He reached out his fingers to the metal handle, and when he pulled it open he was met with a huge gust of wind and a whirling flurry of snow that made Leandra cry out as loudly as before. He quickly pushed it to then jumped at the sound of another voice.

"What is it? What's going on?"

Charlie hadn't heard Ryan make his way from upstairs. The rugby captain glanced suspiciously at Charlie for a moment, then looked at the front door and froze. "What the hell is that?"

Leandra still couldn't talk. Charlie turned back to Ryan and shrugged. "I don't know. Leandra came down here, saw it, and her scream woke me up. That's all I know."

Ryan nodded slowly, scratched at the stubble on his chin, and took a step nearer to the door, his hand outstretched.

Charlie shook his head. "I wouldn't. That storm's horrendous. And you can't see more than a few metres anyway."

Several of Ryan's friends stamped down the stairs and gathered alongside him. Charlie recognized the first one as Jordan, a tall, hard-faced student whose features looked as if they had been pummelled in a scrum one time too many. He wasn't wearing a top, and his pale, athletic torso had the look of Renaissance statue, carved out of marble.

Charlie and Jordan were already acquainted. When Charlie had first joined the school, the other boy had made a beeline for him – eyeballing him, throwing scraps of food in his direction and generally trying to come up with an excuse to make Charlie ask for a beating. Charlie had met his kind before, a lot of times, at a lot of different schools. And once Jordan had realized that Charlie wasn't going to rise to it, he had quickly moved on to more responsive and easily tormented targets.

Jordan's sullen eyes fell on to Charlie and he marched straight over to him. He stood there in nothing but a pair of tracksuit bottoms and studied the scene like a slightly confused Doberman, then he bumped his chest against Charlie's shoulder. Leandra stumbled and Charlie took an involuntary step backwards.

Jordan's nose hovered inches from Charlie's, his breath stale and dry and unpleasant. His pale eyes flickered towards Leandra, lingering on her long legs. "What you been doing, Crim? Trying to get cosy with the girls?"

Charlie shook his head wearily. "I reckon you've had too many bumps to the head. She's so scared she can't even speak."

It was as if someone had punched a syringe of adrenaline into the boy's chest. Jordan's eyes widened under his cherubic curly blond hair and he lunged forwards, his fingers grabbing at Charlie's shirt.

"Come on, then, you criminal! You think you can disrespect me? You think I'm scared of you cause you're some cheap scrawny hood?"

Ryan grabbed Jordan by the arm and hauled

him away. "Pack it in, Jordan. It's nothing to do with him. At least I don't think it is. Look!"

Ryan nodded at the doorway. Most of the assembled boys were ready to pounce on Charlie, but slowly their eyes gravitated to the trail outside the door.

"It's blood, isn't it?" one of them mumbled, a red-haired student called Angus. He was normally one of the more lary of the group, but in the grey light of the lobby he looked like a scared little boy.

A few of the girls from the top floor stumbled into the crowd that was developing. There was a chorus of whimpers and gasps, then a girl called Ellie stepped forwards and gently eased Leandra away from Charlie and into the arms of their group.

For a while nobody spoke. The wind howled and whipped around the hotel's eaves, and somebody's stomach growled morosely. A thin, curly haired girl called Poppy stepped forwards. She had pretty, delicate features and pale skin, and Charlie tried not to notice that her nightgown was almost totally see-through. The hairs on her arm stood up as she put her fingertips on the cold glass. She stood there for a moment before asking the question they were all thinking.

"Whose blood is it?"

Nobody answered her. Poppy moved away from the doorway and Charlie watched as the small circles of condensation from her fingertips faded away. A girl that Charlie thought was called Tara started to cry, ashen tears running down her cheeks to land on the chest of her purple hoodie. Her bottom lip was wobbling, her sobs a few seconds away from hysterics. Ryan moved over to the girl and slipped his arm around her. He looked at the faces around him.

"Where are the teachers?" asked Ryan, turning towards two of his friends.

"Go and have a look, boys. Knock on their doors and tell them there's a problem."

Jordan and another lad – a huge, chunky guy who Charlie thought was called Jacob – thundered away up the stairs.

"Hey, hey! What's all the noise?"

Charlie glanced up to see Stefan staggering down the stairs. His thick blond hair was dishevelled, his eyes still half closed with what was probably a mixture of tiredness and hangover. He yawned, pushed through the mass of teenagers and stopped by the front door. Charlie watched as the carefree smile slipped from his face like a dropped barbell.

"What is it?" asked a voice Charlie recognized. The words were hard and heavily accented, the speaker someone who was used to being listened to.

Charlie's heart sank. He tried to shrink into the shadows as the girl pushed her way through to the door, the same girl who had dug him out of the snow the day before. Her black hair hung down in thick strands and her pale face was alert and curious.

A blanket enveloped her from under her chin to down by her feet, and Charlie found himself wondering if perhaps she and Stefan were more than just colleagues. She probably wasn't any older than Charlie himself and Stefan must have been at least twenty, but from the whispers he'd heard on the ski lifts and in the dining room most of the girls in the school party had their eye on the handsome ski instructor.

The girl looked at the blood through the glass and ran her tongue over her lips.

"A fox, maybe, dragging its food away? A wolf

perhaps? They say they are on the rise again in Germany, but I've never seen them here."

"Wolves? Out there?"

The words came in a whimper from one of the huddles of students that were slowly growing as the last of the school party made their way into the lobby. A thunder of footsteps came from above their heads and Jordan and Jacob thumped back down the stairs.

Jordan's usual leer was gone as he looked back and forth from Ryan to Stefan before finally choosing to give his report to the instructor.

"They're gone. Their rooms are empty, me and Jacob went in. We probably shouldn't have, but Jacob tried the door to Mr Down's room and it just opened. All his stuff's still there, but there's no sign of him. Or Potter. Or Newman. We tried them all."

One of the girls, Chloe, started to cry, the noise low and mournful as it fought against the screech of the wind. Tara tapped away at her glowing phone, swearing at the lack of reception. Ryan looked uncertainly at Stefan as he started to gently guide the group towards the dining room.

"Come on. Let's get a drink, get some coffee

going. I'm sure the teachers will be back in a minute. There must be an explanation for all this."

A few students stepped hesitantly over to where Charlie stood and inspected the red smear before retreating back into the lounge with the others.

After a while, only Charlie and the black-haired Austrian girl were left. She came to stand by him next to the glass. Up close, he realized how striking she was. Her pale grey eyes studied him for a moment and she scratched at the shaved hair on the side of her head. Neither of them spoke. A howling gust of wind broke the silence, and the girl turned to the window and stared at the trail in the snow, her breath fogging around her face like mist.

Chapter Seven

It had gone eleven and the morning outside was still grey and dull, the air thick with snow, the wind so fierce that every now and again the whole hotel seemed to rattle and strain against its foundations.

It felt apocalyptic.

Stefan walked into the dining room just as Tara forced down a reluctant mouthful of dry cereal. As well as the teachers, the Polish girls who had cooked dinner the night before seemed to have gone missing, and the students had been forced to scavenge what they could from the storeroom at the back of the kitchen.

Bran flakes were the only thing that vaguely appealed to Tara, and she'd poured as many as she could face into a chipped bowl and then sat down next to Kelsey and Chloe at one of the tables. There wasn't any milk. Pretty much all of the students had stopped crying now, including those who had tried to act like they just had something in their eye, but whenever Tara pictured the blood by the front door or thought about home, she felt a sharp jolt of fear run through her like electricity.

When she looked up, Stefan was hovering nervously at the bar. He had dressed properly now, in his red ski jacket and trousers that were emblazoned reassuringly with the word *instructor*. He coughed into his hand then looked at the crowd gathered in front of him.

"OK, so the lifts aren't working; I think they've been switched off further down the valley. But even if they were running, this storm is so bad it wouldn't be safe. This wind is too much."

Maybe it was Tara's imagination, but Stefan's normally impeccable English seemed clumsier somehow, his pronunciation a little rougher.

A thin pale arm went up just behind Tara.

"Where's everyone gone? Where are the people that work here? Where are the teachers?"

Tara turned and saw that it had been Poppy that asked the question. She was one of those girls that pretended to be badly behaved, a bit of a rebel, but in reality was really obedient and did exactly as asked. Tara had heard her before in the common room, going on about how she'd given attitude to this teacher and that, how defiant she was. But actually she wasn't at all. Normally she had a smug, mutinous confidence about her, but now she just looked terrified.

Stefan ran a hand over his unruly mop of hair and shook his head.

"Honestly? I don't know. It makes no sense. A lot of the locals left because of the storm, I know that much. But there's no reason for your teachers to not be here, or Martyna and Alicja. I have no idea where they are."

A geeky, dark-skinned kid, who Tara had never really bothered to speak to but thought was called Nico, asked a question from where he was slumped in the corner. "So whose blood was that? Outside the front door? Was it one of the teachers'?"

Stefan flicked a quick glance towards the girl at the bar, the pale, black-haired one who took people out on tours around the valley and didn't seem to have any other expression than a scowl. Tara had fallen out with her on the first day when she had asked her, politely, to carry her bags. The Austrian girl's crass response had sunk the slim chance there might have been of any friendship developing between the two of them.

Stefan shook his head. "No, I don't think so. It was probably just a bird, a rabbit. There's lots of wildlife here. Something caught it, ate it."

"But, Sir, that was a lot of blood. Once, I saw someone get stabbed down on Park Street and he bled a lot, but not as much as that out there."

Stefan sighed and looked in the direction of a squat, confused-looking student nestled among the rugby boys. "You don't have to call me *Sir*, Jacob. I'm just a ski instructor. You're right, though, there was a lot of blood. But it could have been a deer, one that got lost then brought down by something. Maybe somebody went outside, fell, perhaps..."

It was as if Stefan realized the unlikelihood of what he was saying, and he abruptly fell silent.

Tara's words came out before she could stop them. "I want to go home. Can't we just go home?"

Stefan glanced in her direction and smiled reassuringly. "Not right now. The lifts are shut. It's too windy for us to run them – when it's as stormy as this the whole network could come down. That's the only way in or out of here, apart from skiing. And the visibility out there is so bad that you'd get lost before you went ten feet. We just have to wait."

Tara felt tears sting at her eyes. She wanted more than anything to be back at home, at her mum's apartment in Clifton, expensive duvet wrapped around her, hot chocolate steaming away next to her. She wiped at her eyes again with her knuckle. "How long, then? How long till we can go home?"

Stefan shrugged. "Two days. Three at the most. Some of the weather reports reckoned that this was going to be the biggest storm in years, and it built so quickly, but it's not the first time they've said that. I went out a while ago and I found it hard to get beyond the porch. Once you get away from the hotel there must be a metre of fresh snow out there in places, and it's building. But it can't snow forever. Whatever happens, it's not going to stop you going home at the end of the week."

Shiv's voice competed to be heard over a particularly strong gust of wind. "Can't we just ski down? Get some goggles, wrap up warm, take our time and get down to the valley?"

Stefan shook his head slowly. "With the amount

of snow we've had, potential avalanches are going to be everywhere. Normally the ski patrols would get out on the slopes with dynamite to trigger them and make it less dangerous, but nobody's done that. The runs will be brimming with snow. And if you didn't get caught in an avalanche, in a storm like this you'd get lost, even if you had GPS and there was a signal. You could easily lose your way, fall, freeze…"

He raked his eyes over the crowd in front of him. "We're safe here. Warm. We've got food, and each other. We just need to sit tight. We're not in any danger here, as long as we stay inside. A few of you could build a fire, get the hearth going. A day or two and someone will come, or the lifts will be running, for sure. Who knows, your teachers might be back here any minute with some crazy excuse as to where they've all been."

Stefan tried on a zany smile but everybody just stared at him despairingly.

He shook his head slowly. "Look, I'm going to go outside again, into the storm, see if I can find anybody, or spot any lights in the buildings. There's bound to be someone out there. The storm must be keeping them inside."

He nodded towards the black-haired girl at the bar. "Hanna's a guide. She's going to come with me. We'll see what we can find."

Tara had a sudden vision of the two of them heading out of the village, hand in hand, leaving the rest of them as prey for whatever had caused the bloodshed at the front door. At the back of the room a pretty, raven-haired girl called Leandra evidently had the same mental image.

'Don't ... don't leave us. Please."

Stefan shook his head in her direction. "We won't, I promise. We'll take a look around, see what we can find. We won't be long."

The two of them headed out towards the lobby. A few of the other students followed them out of the dining room and there was the sound of several pairs of footsteps climbing the stairs. A moment later there was a howl of wind, the crash of a door flying to and then Stefan and his surly girlfriend were gone.

Across from Tara, Ryan rose slowly to his feet, crossed the room and sat down next to her. He had a white T-shirt on, huge biceps bulging on his bare arms. He stared at Tara for a moment then awkwardly placed his hand on hers.

"Thank you. For not telling Mrs Newman and the others about Monday night. They'd have taken me off the team for sure. Worse maybe."

Tara shrugged. "You know I'd never do anything to hurt you. You're the only good thing that's come out of that shitty school."

She nestled into him, comforted by the solid feel of his chest. "But anyway, nobody would have believed it, even if I'd have told them. Me … and somebody from the *Benedict estate*? Those flats? I don't think so. I mean, I know you don't fit in there, but…"

Ryan nodded and gave her hand a gentle squeeze.

"You're right, I guess. I won't always live there. I know you see past all that. But I'm still grateful you didn't tell them. You OK?"

Tara shook her head slowly.

"Not really. I wish Newman had sent me home yesterday. And I wish more than anything that I'd gone to my mother's chalet in Verbier rather than here."

Chapter Eight

Hanna paused at the edge of the mountain and watched the last of the day slowly slip away. The temperature must have been minus fifteen and dropping. Even with her thick ski jacket, gloves, hat and scarf, Hanna's teeth still chattered inside her skull and she could no longer feel her fingers or toes. The relentless snow and wind burned at the exposed skin round her nose and cheeks, and she felt herself sway forwards and back like a zombie.

But as cold as she was, she didn't want to make her way back to the hotel.

Not yet.

She wiped the ice away from her goggles and stared down over the edge of the ravine, into the chasm of whirling snow. Somewhere down there, through the cloud and fog and ice, hundreds of feet from where she stood, was the foot of the valley and the nearest glimmer of civilisation.

But Hanna wouldn't find the answers she longed for down there.

Kaldgellan had never been the busiest of resorts, tucked away as it was from the rest of the world, but that had always been part of its attraction. In winter, the only way up to the mountain range was on the gondola, and there wasn't much in the way of après ski unless you liked hanging out in a gloomy bar with the local drunks and a selection of dusty, fading mounted heads. There was usually little more than a handful of visitors at a time, a school party or two and a few walkers. No normal teenager would have wanted to spend their time up here, cut off from the rest of the world. But Hanna had given up any pretence of normality a long time ago.

She felt a sudden urge to turn and run, to dash back to the hotel, away from the unseen eyes that she felt sure were watching her. But she fought it, wrestled against it, trying to ignore the sense that the life had been sucked out of the village overnight, and all the residents along with it.

Stefan and Hanna had spent their day going from hotel to shop to lift to residence, and they had found nobody. They had knocked on doors, peered through windows, hammered on grilles and shutters, and tried every house they could get to. But if there was anyone home, they didn't want to be found.

They had looked into car windows, checked the lift stations, even squinted up into the cable cars that swung to and fro in the screeching wind. But every time it had been the same.

Nothing.

When she had been little, Hanna had heard the story of the Mary Celeste and she had always been fascinated by the tale. Now she felt like she had wandered right into the middle of the fable and stepped aboard the famous ghost ship.

She had sent Stefan back to reassure the students at the hotel, but the truth was there was nothing to tell them. The village was deserted and Hanna had no idea why. But she had the surest, keenest sense that it wouldn't be long until she found out.

She thought back to Matthias's garbled warning of the day before, a nonsensical stream of frightened words, something about how the mountains weren't what they seemed.

Somehow, she'd known he was speaking the truth.

Matthias had told her to leave. And yet here she was.

And perhaps it was her imagination, but every time the wind fell, every time the howl across the drifts lessened, the faintest of sounds seemed to come to her ears: chatter, voices, scuttling, the quick fall of feet.

Something was out there, waiting. Something that had brought Hanna back here, after all she'd been through. Something terrible.

Hanna stole one last glance at the valley far below, then turned back towards the hotel, wondering if tonight she might finally learn the answers to the questions that had haunted her for as far back as she could remember.

Chapter Nine

They were sitting in the hotel lounge, the last of the light long gone from the sky, when a dull, insistent pounding on the door stopped Stefan mid-sentence. Several of the girls screamed. One of the rugby boys swore, the word loaded with fright.

And then it came again.

Thump. Thump. Thump.

Stefan looked like he was on the edge of exhaustion. He had stood by the fire, dripping on the carpet, hollowly reassuring them that everything would be all right. Tomorrow, he said, somebody would be on their way. Tomorrow the internet would be back and they'd all laugh about what had happened.

Charlie sat at the back of the dimly lit room, measuring the disbelief on the faces of the students around him. He was pretty sure that Stefan himself didn't believe the words he was saying.

Then the noise had cut him dead.

Thump. Thump. Thump.

It sounded to Charlie like a bear's paw knocking on the glass; a mindless, heavy pounding.

"Oh no, please... Is it ... is it the teachers?" A girl called Amy whispered the words from among the pinched, scared faces gathered in the dowdy Alpine bar. She rose out of her chair, looked towards the hallway then quickly sank back down.

There was a scrape as Ryan pushed his chair back, but Stefan held up his hand decisively. "No. I'll go."

Stefan started to walk hesitantly to the lobby, dark rings under his eyes. When Charlie thought about it later, when he considered what had happened to the students who had been sitting just next to him against the glass of the dining-room windows, he couldn't have said why he got up and went after Stefan. But when he looked back later that night, he realized that it had been the most important decision of his life.

By the time he got to the entrance that led to the lobby, Stefan's fingertips were on the door that led out into the storm. The guide, Hanna, was standing next to Charlie, an uncertain light in her grey eyes.

Charlie jerked as Ryan's large hand came to rest on his shoulder. The rugby captain pushed him gently to one side so that he could see what was happening.

Stefan looked back for a moment at them, his face confused.

"There's nobody there. Nothing."

Charlie studied the television static of the world outside, his mouth dry. Nothing moved beyond the door but a constant, steady fall of snow. Stefan turned back to face the blizzard.

And then the whole door blew inwards in an explosion of snow, glass, and ice. Stefan screamed as the debris engulfed him and everything seemed to slow down.

Charlie saw something dart into the lobby – a tall, thin figure, fast and dark. It moved so quickly that he barely registered it. One second Stefan was there amidst a feverish cloud of debris, the next the shape wrapped itself around him. Charlie just had time to make out a set of dirty, taloned fingers folding themselves into the thick mop of the instructor's hair.

Then both Stefan and the intruder vanished back out into the storm. Nobody had time to even move.

At Charlie's shoulder, Ryan was shouting the

instructor's name frantically. Hanna was frozen stock still, her eyes wide with disbelief.

And then there were more screams.

This time they came from inside the room at their backs, coupled with the sound of more shattering glass. Charlie turned to look back into the dining room, two frenzied girls pushing past him. He stared past them and tried to process what he saw.

All around the room the curtains were billowing in amidst a blizzard of glistening shards of ice and snow and quick figures were darting in, embracing the students nearest to the windows and stealing them back out into the storm. Other members of the party, those lucky enough to be sitting away from the windows, streamed past Charlie in the direction of the lobby, faces pale with terror.

Charlie watched as a screaming, red-haired girl clung to the arm of a chair by her fingernails before being torn away and dragged out into the darkness. He couldn't make out what it was that took her.

He wasn't sure he wanted to.

He was about to turn and run himself when he noticed that over in the corner of the room, by the forgotten television screen, a dishevelled, grey figure had pinned down another of the students who hadn't moved quickly enough.

Charlie knew who the pounding fists and kicking legs belonged to.

Her name was Kelsey and she was a tall, olive-skinned girl that caught the same bus as Charlie and scowled across at him every morning. She still wore the same pair of checked Vans that Charlie had seen propped up on the seat in front of her on the long journeys to school.

One taloned hand clutched the girl's dressing gown, another was tangled in her short dark hair. Charlie couldn't see the face of the intruder because it was buried in the folds of the dressing gown by Kelsey's neck, but its head moved up and down frantically, ravenously. As if it was savaging the girl, biting at her. Ragged swathes of dirty, faded material seemed to cover her attacker, loose edges catching in the wind.

Charlie watched as Kelsey's frenzied movements grew less and less urgent, the fight seeping out of her. A long, thick stream of blood started to run down the patterned material of her dressing gown to pool on the grubby carpet at her feet.

A hand grabbed Charlie's arm and he heard himself cry out. Hanna pushed past him, towards the bar, her hand scrabbling for something that hung amidst the beer glasses above the till. She grabbed the front of his hoodie and shouted into his face, her nose inches from his.

"Move! Go!"

She ran out of the room and turned left to scramble up the stairs. Charlie stared for a heartbeat more, then tore himself away from the horror in the dining room and followed Hanna. His feet worked automatically, the stairs moving under him like a conveyor belt, his mind frozen and numb.

As he neared the first-floor landing, he chanced a glance backwards. Students stumbled this way and that, fleeing from the dining room, trying to put as much space between themselves and what was happening in there as they could. Charlie watched as something slipped in through the glass in the shattered lobby door and lashed out at one of the students, Amy, catching her by the arm and dragging her screaming. Charlie caught Amy's eyes for a second, saw the pleading and terror there.

Then he turned and ran.

He didn't have time to register how many students were on the landing with Hanna. Ten maybe, a dozen.

One of them, Tara, was shouting and crying. Jordan looked like he was about to throw up, chanting feverish words to anyone who would listen.

"What the hell are they? What's happening? What are they? What's happening?"

Without a word, Hanna pushed past Charlie and started to run along the corridor. She didn't look like she wanted to be followed, but out of instinct more than anything else he turned and ran after her, aware that some of the others were doing the same behind him. There was more screaming from the bottom floor, more sounds of forced entry into the rooms below.

Charlie ran up one flight of stairs after Hanna, then another. His heart was pounding in his chest, his mind a blank. By the time he caught up with her, Hanna was standing at the end of a corridor on the top floor, one hand clenched around a hatch above her head. She waited until several more students had arrived, then she spoke quickly and quietly.

"I don't know what the hell is going on but I'm

not staying in here. I'm going out on to the roof. It will be freezing. But I'm not staying in this hotel. If you come with me, you need to be silent and you need to stay down. If you can't do that I'll throw you off the roof myself. Understand?"

Nobody spoke. They were all too out of breath or too scared to speak so much as a word.

Taking the silence as agreement, Hanna reached up, pulled the hatch down and released the stairs that led up on to the roof. She took four quick steps and was gone. Charlie watched as Ryan helped Tara up ahead of him then clambered up himself. Another figure climbed up. Then another. Charlie knew some of them. Poppy. Chloe. Ellie. Jordan. Shiv. There were a couple more, but he didn't know their names.

He was last to climb up the metal steps. By the time his turn came he was shaking, his eyes constantly flicking back the way they had come, expecting to see a dark shape slip into the corridor and then launch itself at him. He pulled himself up the steps and found Hanna waiting for him. She shoved him to one side without a word and, as quietly as she could, pulled the cord on the hatch and retracted the stairs.

Charlie glanced around.

They were on a small, flat rooftop, the barest sliver of a moon visible through a barrage of snow that was coming at them almost horizontally. A small huddle of students gathered in the middle of the space, as far away from the knee-high walls on all sides as it was possible to get.

Some of them were wearing pyjamas. One wore a dressing gown, while Ryan and another of the rugby team were just dressed in T-shirts and tracksuit bottoms.

And Hanna had been right, it was beyond freezing. Charlie was only wearing his hoodie and jeans, and he felt his teeth start to chatter.

He watched as Hanna pushed past him on her haunches and made her way to the edge of the roof. She paused there, lifting herself up so that she could see over the edge of the low wall. Charlie pulled up his hood and paced after her, suddenly aware from the numbing cold in his toes that all he had on his feet were socks.

He put his hands on the low wall. Hanna glanced across at him, but didn't say a word. Charlie stared up at the sky, the thick swathes of snow driving across on the wind, then he looked downwards at the drifts that had settled three floors below.

In the falling snow, just visible in the darkness, a score of quick figures darted here and there, like wolves on the hunt. Some were huddled over their victims, who struggled and writhed beneath them in the snow. Charlie pictured Kelsey and the creature that had caught her in the dining room, and he tasted warm blood in his mouth as he bit into his lip. Other shapes dragged their prey away through the blizzard, out of sight. From far away, Charlie heard himself swear. He turned to Hanna.

"What ... what are they? What the hell is going on?"

Hanna stared at him for a heartbeat then shook her head slowly. She didn't seem scared, but her grey eyes were wide, her breath coming in quick shallow bursts. "I don't know. But I'm not staying here."

She turned and darted back to the others. Charlie moved as if to follow her, but something caught his eye.

Far below, near the entrance to the hotel, a lone

figure stood – unmoving, long dark hair whipping this way and that in the breeze. For some reason it reminded Charlie of a conductor, a still figure in charge of the chaos all around it. He couldn't make out any more than a shape, a single point of calm among the storm, but there was no mistaking it. As if the figure sensed it was being watched, it started to turn slowly and deliberately in Charlie's direction.

Before he saw its face, Charlie ducked down and scuttled after Hanna, his socks sopping in the thick snow.

One of the rugby boys, Malachi, was crying, his face hidden behind his fingers. An athletic, dark-skinned girl called Shiv pulled him close to her. Tara sat huddled into Ryan, his arm around her like a shield. There were no more than a dozen or so of them in the small group.

Charlie found himself wondering if they were the only ones left alive.

Tara pulled her face away from Ryan's sopping shirt. "I want to get away, please, please, I need to get home, I shouldn't be here, please!"

Her voice became higher, hysterical, and Hanna

glared at Ryan. "You need to shut her up, or I'll do it. Right now."

Ryan nodded numbly and pulled Tara's face against his chest, muffling her sobs. Hanna stared at the girl venomously for a moment and Charlie found himself thinking back to their meeting on the mountain, wondering if there was a reason for the hostile way she seemed to treat everyone she ran into.

Hanna raked her eyes over the rest of the group. "We can't stay here. We'll be dead from exposure in minutes if we stay in this storm. I'm going to get inside. Not here, somewhere else. You can come with me if you must, but if you make a sound, if you make those things hear us, whatever they are, I'll leave you down there alone."

Malachi looked at her imploringly. "Please. We just want to get away."

Hanna nodded. "I know. I do, too. So I need you to do exactly what I say."

Chapter Ten

Hanna led them over the side wall at the back of the hotel, then down a set of fire stairs that zigzagged down to the ground below. She didn't wait to see if the others were behind her. Instead she darted across the empty space behind the hotel, in the direction of the lift station.

Charlie was next in line and he followed her as she scrambled along in front of the row of deserted shops and cafés at the back of the hotel, keeping as low as he could. He had no idea where they were going but he kept close to their guide, only looking behind once to see if the others were still there. He counted four of them trailing behind him before he had to carry on for fear of losing sight of Hanna.

He rounded the corner of the village's lone ski-hire shop and barged straight into her. She was crouched down at the side of the building, her eyes fixed somewhere in the distance. She ignored Charlie and fumbled around in her pocket for something. She swore in German, struggled some more, then pulled out a bristling set of keys. She pressed down on one of them and twenty metres away Charlie saw two sets of lights glitter orange through the falling snow before blinking off.

Without a word, Hanna stood and started to run.

Charlie struggled to keep up with her as she sprinted across the open space between the back of the shop and the parking lot in the distance. As he ran, he saw the shape of a minibus come into focus through the darkness.

Hanna half fell in the thick snow, recovered, then reached the minibus and put her back against it, fumbling with the keys again. She pressed a button, reached out and gently pulled the side door open, sliding it back just enough for a person to slip through.

"Whose is this?" Charlie gasped against burning lungs.

Hanna glanced sideways at him. She seemed barely out of breath. "It belongs to the hotel, but it's used by anyone who needs it. They always keep the keys behind the bar, for running things and people to the lifts and back. I just hope it starts."

Hanna stepped on to the minibus and ducked down by the steering wheel. Charlie climbed up and dropped down in the first seat he came to. He watched anxiously as other figures started to make their way up the steps. First Poppy. Then Ryan and Tara. He counted seven of them apart from himself and Hanna.

The last one to step on to the minibus was Jordan. He didn't look at Charlie as he ducked down in the aisle next to him. Hanna stared across at his pale, stony face. "Is that it? Are you the last?"

Jordan seemed to come out of a daze. "Yeah. Yeah, I think so."

He took a deep breath, rubbed at his hair, frozen like steel wire and looked back towards the doorway. "I think … I think maybe there were some others but I'm not sure they saw where we were going."

He paused, shook his head. "Shit, I think I lost them. I should have waited, shouldn't I? I think that was my fault." He wiped at his nose and lowered his head, then started to shiver and sob.

Shiv reached out a hand from the seat next to him and rested it on Jordan's shoulder. "It isn't your fault.

Nobody knows what the hell is going on. Try not to think about it."

Shiv glanced across at Hanna, sitting low in the driver's seat. "What are we doing? You going to start this thing?"

Hanna shook her head slowly, looked through the driver's door at the storm, then sank down into the aisle and made her way to the seat in front of Charlie's, near where the rest of the group had congregated.

"For now we stay here. I don't know if the minibus will even start. I don't think its been used for a few weeks. And I don't want to let those things know where we are."

Ryan swore loudly, his breath fogging out in front of him in the half-light.

"What were they? I saw one of them drag Jacob out through the window like he was nothing. I feel like I'm dreaming. Did anyone else see that? Christ, Jacob weighed sixteen stone. It'd take three of us to lift him like that. Whatever it was that came in through the window pulled him outside as if he was lighter than my little brother. What the hell is going on?"

Hanna ignored Ryan's question and glanced

around the group. "Can anyone drive?'

Charlie nodded. "A little. I've driven a little, tractors, cars. I don't have a licence, but I can drive."

Hanna scrutinized him for a moment then handed him the keys. They felt hot and heavy in his hand. When she spoke, her words were barely a whisper. "If we need to go, you start this thing and get it moving. Go and have a look now, check that you know where the key goes."

Charlie nodded and moved down the aisle, into the driver's seat, glad to have a purpose. He put his foot on the clutch and played with the gearbox. Finally he put the key in the ignition, checked it turned and clicked it back off. From high up in the driver's seat, he could see the tree-lined road winding away down the hill towards the lift station, a deep layer of snow hiding where the markings should be.

He left the key dangling in the ignition and crept back down the aisle. A couple of the group had commandeered discarded jackets and coats that had been left in the minibus. Ryan pulled on a hoodie that was far too small for him and passed a coat over to one of the girls. Charlie reached down and pulled off his soaking socks. His toes were painfully numb and if he had to run again it was going to be a problem. Hanna saw what he was doing, reached past him and handed him a pair of furry boots that had been left on the seat behind. They were badly worn, and at least a size too small, but Charlie managed to squeeze his foot into the fleecy lining.

A few seats away, Tara wiped at her eyes and shook her head. "Can't we just go now? Why are we sitting here? Why are we waiting for those things to find us?"

Hanna stared at her coldly. "What if we start the minibus and it doesn't work? What if those things are as fast as they are strong? It's not a chance I'm willing to take. For now we just need to stay still. We're dry, we're safe in here, and I don't want to send those things an invite to find us."

Tara stared back at her.

"Who put you in charge? Just because you spend your day bossing people around on the mountain doesn't mean that you can tell us all what to do."

For a moment Charlie thought Hanna was going to swing for Tara, then she shook her head and swore in German. "I didn't ask you to follow me. Any of you. And if you don't like what I'm doing

81

you're welcome to leave. There's the door."

Tara followed Hanna's line of vision and sniffed. "Maybe I will."

The wind rocked the coach gently to and fro. Malachi started sobbing again. "What is going on? What were those things? Where did they take the others? I saw one of them grab Amy by the hair, and just drag her along the floor. It looked like … like…"

He started to cry harder, his words lost among a series of choked sobs. Hanna shook her head. "Pull yourself together. If those things hear you, you'll draw them over here. Then you'll be just the same as your friends."

Charlie looked out at the storm. The snow seemed to be falling heavier than ever. Jordan rubbed at his eyes and looked around the group.

"Malachi's right, though, what were they? They were like something out of a film. I'm sure they were … shit, I saw one of them *eating* one of the girls. Like she was a burger. Proper eating her."

In the aisle, Shiv nodded. "I saw that, too. Like demons, or vampires, or—"

Hanna swore and cut her dead. "There's no such

thing. There isn't! I don't know what they were, some psychos in masks maybe. So we need to—"

Ellie's voice came from the back of the vehicle, sounding on the verge of hysteria. "Oh my God, there's one of them down there, near the shops. Look, it's got one of the girls. I can't watch, I can't…"

Hanna scuttled down the aisle and slid alongside Poppy and Ellie on one of the seats on the right-hand side of the bus. Charlie followed her, some of the group crowding around him. Hanna slid slowly upwards, so that her eyes just rose above the windowsill to let her see what was happening outside.

Charlie did the same and instantly wished he hadn't.

About thirty feet from the back of the minibus, just before the point where the falling snow made visibility fade to nothing, one of the creatures had paused in the snow. It looked back over its shoulder furtively then glanced down at the girl at its feet.

Charlie recognized her. He thought her name was Chloe. She was a bubbly, cheerful girl that was often on duty in the common room, telling others to put their rubbish in the bin, to keep the place tidy, to respect the school facilities. The kind of girl that always did the right thing.

Now she lay slumped on her back, eyes wide, snow settling on her face. Her dressing gown had fallen open and the T-shirt underneath had ridden up so that the pale skin of her belly was exposed.

Ellie turned to the others. "Shouldn't we... Shouldn't we help her?"

Hanna shook her head slowly. "*Nein*. Not yet. Not until we know a little more."

Jordan swore quietly. "She was right behind me. Then when I looked back, she was gone."

Chloe's attacker stood up as if stretching the muscles in his back and lifted his head up to the sky. He looked almost like a normal man, short, stocky, bald-headed. He was dressed in a ragged pair of worker's dungarees over a tattered, faded shirt, like the attendants who ran the lifts on the slopes. There were dirty, brown stained bandages around his hands and on one of his arms, as if he had cut himself on some machinery. But there was something wrong with his face and his mouth.

The man's features were jagged, angular, feral and far too pale to be normal. His mouth seemed too wide for his face somehow. And maybe it was a trick of the light or the storm, but Charlie thought he saw gums lined with jagged teeth, far larger and thicker than those of a normal person.

Ellie's eyes were wide, frantic. "We need to help her!"

Hanna shook her head. "No, we don't."

The thing paused in its stretch, looked down at Chloe's still form. It seemed to Charlie as if she was alive but too scared to move, too scared to do anything but stare, her twitching pupils betraying the fact that she was conscious. The creature studied her for a moment longer before it lunged its face down towards the skin of her belly, its teeth slashing this way and that.

Blood started to splatter on the snow, and Chloe's limbs twisted and jerked as if she was on strings.

A few seats down from Charlie, Jordan started swearing frantically.

Hanna flickered round, her voice little more than a hiss. "*Nein*! Shut up! Shut up!"

Poppy whispered at the back of the bus, her words

full of despair. "Oh no … it heard us. It knows we're here."

Charlie looked back out of the window then ducked down. The thing had stopped feeding and it stood stock still, staring at the minibus, its head cocked to one side like a dog. Charlie had only gotten the briefest of glimpses, but even so there was no missing the slick of blood that ran down the creature's mouth and chin.

Hanna slid back into the aisle, moved halfway down the minibus and looked around. "Nobody move. Nobody make a sound."

She glanced across at Charlie. "Charlie. That's your name isn't it? I need you to make your way along the coach, to the driver's seat. Slide into the foot well. But don't start the engine unless I say."

Charlie did as he was told. As he made his way along the aisle, he saw the faces of the other students, eyes wide with terror, backs against the inside of the bus, their shallow breath dancing around them like mist.

Charlie made it to the front, and then slid into the foot well. Just before he sank down, he caught a quick glimpse of the creature through the door opposite the driver's seat. It stood perfectly still, eyes fixed on the bus.

"Nobody move," Hanna repeated.

Charlie watched her lift her head slowly above the glass, trying to work out what the creature was doing without being seen.

There was a thud as Hanna slammed back down on to the seat. Then a long, low, hungry howl echoed around the car park.

Chapter Eleven

Hanna heard the words fall from her lips at the awful howl, felt the eyes of the others jerk in her direction. "*Scheisse*, it saw me! It knows we're here! Charlie, start the engine, start it, start it now!"

Charlie scrambled up out of the foot well, turned the key and Hanna heard the heavy engine start to grumble and labour. Then it died. Charlie tried it again, only for it to fade once more. Hanna made her way along the coach, her eyes darting out into the storm.

The creature that had savaged Chloe was running towards the coach. Other shapes were approaching too, in the distance, just past the shops.

Charlie turned the key again, the panic in his voice palpable. "There's more, three of them! They're coming!"

Hanna arrived at his shoulder, her hand on

the seat. On the fifth turn of the key the ignition caught and the whole coach started to rumble and quake as it fought to get warm against the freezing night air.

Hanna gripped his arm, trying to ignore the ominous figures approaching through the blizzard. "Drive! Get us out of here!"

Charlie let the clutch slip and stamped on the throttle. The minibus lurched then fell back. He swore, released the handbrake, then stamped on the pedal again. The vehicle started to move, then froze again. Hanna could hear the wheels spinning uselessly as they tried to get purchase.

Charlie slammed his hand on the steering wheel and looked back at Hanna. "It's stuck, it's stuck fast! I can't get it moving, the snow's too deep!"

There were screams and yells from the back and two heavy thuds as something climbed on to the roof.

Shiv's voice echoed off the walls. "They're here! They're on the bus! Please, drive, somebody drive!"

Charlie stamped on the throttle again, the minibus refusing to obey. "We're not going anywhere. I can't get out of the snow!"

Hanna heard heavy footsteps above her head. "*Nein, nein!*"

She pointed down at the gearbox, then stared at Charlie. "What do we do? What do we do?"

Charlie put his hand on the stick and looked back up at her. "Reverse?"

Hanna nodded frantically. "Slam it into reverse and stamp on the throttle as hard as you can!"

Charlie engaged the clutch, ground the gears and forced it into reverse. Then he stamped down on the pedal and closed his eyes.

There was the harsh sound of the tyres searching for purchase then suddenly the bus flew backwards. Hanna lost her grip on the back of Charlie's chair and found herself tumbling back down the aisle.

When she heaved herself up, the world around them was moving, the car park a blur. A set of tyre prints unravelled themselves in front of the window as the minibus gathered speed. Behind Hanna, the other students screamed and shouted. Through the side mirror, she saw a figure ram into the back of the vehicle and vanish under the winter tyres, the minibus lurching upwards over the obstacle. Hanna tried not to dwell on the noise that accompanied the impact.

Charlie's voice dragged her back into the world. He glanced back over his shoulder, his hands on the wheel. "Where am I going?"

Hanna caught a glimpse of herself in the windscreen. A thin line of blood ran from her scalp over the shaved hair on the side of her head down towards her ear. She was so full of adrenaline she hadn't even noticed.

Hanna turned, looked along the length of the bus. "Don't stop. And don't go forwards. We'll never make it far that way. Keep going straight backwards. Aim at the ski-hire shop, as hard and as fast as you can!"

Charlie stared back at her. "We'll just smash into it!"

She nodded. "That's the plan. The walls are thin, we'll go straight through. Keep the wheel straight and go. As fast as you can!"

She looked back at the other passengers. "Everybody away from the back of the bus! Hold on tight and get down!"

Hanna's heart was pounding. She glanced up at the rear-view mirror, saw the side of the shop coming closer and closer. The red arrow of the speedometer flickered past forty, heading to fifty.

Then they hit.

While Charlie was flung forwards on to the steering wheel, Hanna threw herself into the two chairs behind the driver's seat, cushioning her from the worst of the impact. There was a huge thundering crash, like an explosion, and Hanna's world became a mass of screaming and pain and twisting metal.

Hanna wasn't sure how long it was before she staggered up from where she'd landed. She looked backwards and saw that they had gone straight through the side of the shop, so that the front of the minibus protruded out into the car park as if the ski-hire shop had swallowed the back half.

She scrambled up and fixed her eyes on Ryan, her voice loud above the shudder and rumble of the engine. "You, get that back door open. Now!"

Ryan struggled with the handle and shook his head desperately. "It won't! The back's smashed in! The doors won't budge!"

Behind her, Hanna heard a pained cough. Charlie's body was sprawled over the steering wheel and he couldn't seem to lift himself. It would only be a matter of seconds until the things from outside made their way in. And Hanna couldn't afford having anyone along that might slow them down.

Before she knew it, she'd somehow made a different choice to the one she was contemplating. She dragged him up by the collar from his seat towards the sliding doors, like a dog on a lead. Others were scrabbling through the gap in front of them and Hanna pushed Charlie down the step.

They emerged into a wreckage of ski poles, collapsed walls and broken mannequins.

The back end of the minibus had gone clean through the wall of the shop, and almost into the off-licence next door. Wires hung from the ceiling, smoke and dust filled the air, and the dying engine groaned and clicked desperately. Hanna stumbled on to the bottom step and slipped on a railing of fallen coats and trousers.

The other students milled around the minibus, dazed, uncertain. Hanna reached down and retrieved a steel hockey stick off the floor then spun round as somebody started screaming.

The noise came from Poppy.

She was on the floor near the end of the minibus and something had hold of her leg. Hanna moved closer and saw that long, thin fingers had hold of her by the ankle, dragging her slowly under the coach. As she watched, the bottom half of one leg slipped from view and Poppy screamed again, loud and frantic.

"Please! No! It's biting me! Get it off, get it..."

Her screams grew louder and louder, and Malachi took hold of her hands and started to try to pull her free. Hanna scrabbled over the debris and smashed the hockey stick down again and again, hammering the arm of the creature. Poppy cried out and jerked her leg free. Hanna hit at the pale fingers once more then backed away hurriedly.

She didn't have time to wonder what it was, or try to piece together what was happening. For now, her mind was fixed only on survival.

The bottom of one leg of Poppy's grey sweat pants was dark with blood, dripping off her bare foot on to the floor below. She wiped at her eyes and swore. "I can't walk, I—"

Shiv lifted Poppy up and put her arm around her. "I've got you. You're OK."

Shiv glanced up at Hanna, waiting for direction. For a moment Hanna considered running out into the night, leaving them to fend for themselves. Before she could come to a decision, noises came from outside, scrapes, footsteps. Hanna caught Charlie's eye then turned her head towards the back of the shop.

"This way. Quickly!"

She turned and ran, still not sure if she wanted the others to follow her or not.

Chapter Twelve

Shiv opened her eyes, coughed and experienced a nauseous wave of images from the night before, an unstoppable tide. She wiped at her nose, held back a stream of tears and tried to distinguish the shapes huddled round her in the tiny room.

Her voice was a dry croak in her ears. "What time is it?"

Across from her, Charlie's face shimmered into view as he squinted down at his battered watch and pressed the button that made it illuminate. "Six-fifty."

Somebody moaned in the darkness. Whether it was from lack of sleep, an injury or just plain fear, Shiv wasn't sure.

Hanna's voice whispered somewhere to her left. "Nearly dawn. And I can't hear those things out there any more."

Slowly, Shiv's world started to fill with slivers of

light as the blackness gave way to grey. She glanced left and right, saw Malachi on one side, Ryan on the other.

Her friends.

Back home, she trained with them in the gym most days, spotting each other, pushing each other, throbbing hip-hop bouncing off the walls while the three of them competed to see who could lift the most.

And last night she almost watched them die.

She swore quietly, struggling to accept what she'd seen, and heard her words echo in the gloom. "We're alive. We're still alive."

A few feet away, Hanna sighed wearily. "For now. The storm is still fierce out there, but I can't hear anything else. And I can't hear those things any more."

Shiv closed her eyes and focused on the noises from the world outside. The wind was whipping around the sides of the derelict building, smashing into the shutters, rattling the rotten wood of the windows. But that was all she could make out.

As hard as she tried to stop herself, Shiv found

her mind slipping back to the horrific events of the night before.

After Charlie had rammed the minibus halfway through the ski shop, Hanna had directed them first through the back of the store then out into the night. She'd run the small group down one alley, then another, to a small, two-storey building with faded wooden panelling. The windows were boarded up, the paintwork on the door chipped and battered, and a chain and padlock wound around the handle. Hanna had shoved the end of the hockey stick behind the chain and started to pull.

"Malachi, Jordan, help me with this!"

The rugby boys had put their combined weight on to the end of the stick and pulled down until the latch popped off the old wooden frame, bringing the screws with it.

Hanna had glanced over her shoulder, jerked open the door and ushered them in. Once they were all inside she'd wound the freed chain around the inside handles and started to scrabble around near the doorway. It had been almost pitch black in the building, the air cold and musty and damp. Somebody had coughed and been rewarded with a hiss from Hanna, who had still been down on her knees. After a few seconds there had been a click and light had seeped into the gloom.

Averting her eyes, Shiv had just been able to make out an old wind-up lantern clutched close to Hanna's chest. Its weak glow had been enough to reveal that they were in a large, open space, with a battered desk in one corner and a high, cobwebbed ceiling above their heads. The place looked like it hadn't been stepped into for years.

Hanna had dimmed the light so that only the weakest glow was emitted as she'd guided them up a rickety set of wooden stairs to a small, panelled room, closing the door behind them.

And they had been there ever since, nobody daring to speak more than a few words.

Now, in the weak dawn light, Charlie put his hand over his mouth to suppress a yawn and whispered in Hanna's direction. Shiv barely knew anything about him, apart from his questionable reputation, but if not for his quick thinking the night before she wasn't sure how many of them would still be breathing.

"What is this place?"

Hanna took a deep breath, let it out again. "It's

an old hostel, from the seventies. Kaldgellan used to get more visitors in the past, but when it got less popular they shut the hostel down. It's stayed here ever since, boarded up and empty."

Shiv's eyes stayed locked on the spiky foreign guide. More fingers of light started to filter through a vent in the wall above their heads, so that she could just make out the jagged edges of Hanna's black hair, the angles of her face. Although she'd led them to safety, there was a cold distance about the Austrian girl, as if those that she had found herself huddled up with were little more than an inconvenience.

Shiv found herself wondering how trustworthy Hanna really was.

Between the gaps in their conversation, the silence felt endless in the darkness, and before long Shiv's question filled the void. "How did you know about this place? Don't you just work here through the winter like Stefan?"

Hanna leaned her head to one side, studying Shiv, then she shook her head slowly. "*Nein*. I was born here. I lived in Kaldgellan for the first few years of my life. My brother, he was much older than me, and when this place closed down he and his friends used it as a ... how do you say it? A den? When I was little he showed me. There's a *verstauen*, a stash by the door, always there, a lantern, candles, some sleeping bags. My brother would bring me here with some of the other children in the village and we'd hide, play. But soon after that our family moved away from here altogether."

Shiv pictured Hanna's life in the remote resort in its secluded corner of the Austrian Alps, far away from any town or bright lights. It made Bristol seem like a throbbing metropolis by comparison, and she wondered what kind of teenager would choose to return to such a desolate, deserted place.

The same thing had occurred to Charlie, and he turned in Hanna's direction. "Why did you come back here?"

A look passed over her face, a flicker of uncertainty. "Something happened here. Something that changed my life. I had to see this place again. I had to put it to rest in my mind and the only way to do that was to come back."

Her words were enigmatic, but before Shiv could ask her any more there was a sniff from the other side of the room, and Tara's voice joined the conversation. "And now you're never going to leave this horrible place. What is this room? It stinks."

Although Tara and Ryan had tried to keep their relationship a secret, Shiv had known about it from the start. Despite Shiv's initial uncertainty, there was a nicer side to Tara, one that Ryan brought to the surface, buried underneath the pampering and the entitlement.

From the hostility in Hanna's voice, it seemed she had already taken a strong dislike to Tara. "What's your name?"

Tara leaned her head to the side and gave Hanna a look loaded with animosity. "Tara."

"All you've done since I met you, Tara, is bitch, moan, cry and complain. This room was used by guests to dry their wet ski clothes and boots. It's warm and it's insulated, so the noise of your whining won't carry outside. But you don't have to stay here. In fact, I'd prefer it if you left. And if you don't shut up I'm going to throw you out to those things."

"What … what were they? What the hell were they?"

Shiv reckoned it was Ellie that had asked the question, the same words that had been uttered again and again during the endless night.

And as with every time before, no one had an answer.

Somebody snored then coughed. A particularly strong gust of wind hammered a shutter to and fro on the other side of the building. It had been doing that all night long. Shiv closed her eyes, images from the night before drifting in the void. A pair of black-checked Vans, blood spattering the canvas. Angus's eyes, shot through with horror and shock, a spidery creature pulling him slowly out into the storm.

Next to her, Ellie started to shake. Shiv reached out and hugged her close, sleep drawing her downwards.

Some time later Tara's voice echoed in the darkness, the sound jerking Shiv awake. "I'm hungry. And uncomfortable."

There was a sharp intake of breath to Shiv's left, but before Hanna could bite Tara's head off, somebody started to cry in the corner.

Poppy.

"I feel sick. That thing … it bit me. It hurts like hell. I think it's still bleeding and it hurts, it hurts so bad. Do you … do you think I'm going to die?"

"No. Not from that, anyway."

Shiv wasn't sure how reassuring Poppy would find Hanna's blunt response.

The silence dragged on again, and Shiv found herself wrestling with her emotions, telling herself she had to hold it together for the sake of the group. Figures took shape amidst the grey. Ryan's arm, curled around Tara like a branch. Jordan's pale face, eyes dark-rimmed and haunted. Poppy's ravaged leg, stretched out in front of her uselessly.

In her life back home, Shiv had her eyes set on being a paramedic, the A-levels she'd chosen and the universities she was considering all part of her long-term plan. She'd even taken first-aid courses, another selling point on her personal statement that might catch the eye of an admissions tutor. In the darkness, Shiv cast a wary glance at Poppy's mauled ankle.

Hanna was right. Poppy wouldn't die, at least not from blood loss. But if a dog had done that, or some other wild animal, she would have needed jabs, antibiotics.

And the creatures that had burst into the hotel were something much more terrifying.

After what felt like the longest time, Hanna

sighed. "We need to move. I'm not sure, but I think those things have gone. They've been howling and yelling all night, but I can't hear them any more. What time is it?"

Charlie checked his watch again. "Eight-fifty."

Hanna yawned and nodded.

"Yesterday, when Stefan and I explored the village, there was no sign of those things. And at least in the daylight we'd be able to see them coming."

Tara's pale features took shape in the gloom. "You're going to … to go out there?"

Across from Shiv, Hanna stood and stretched, and Ryan glanced up at her.

"Is it safe? I mean, do you think they'll still be out there, whatever the hell they were?"

Nobody answered, and the building creaked and groaned against the force of the gale. Hanna kneeled back down among them as if she was at confession, and wiped at her face.

When she spoke, Shiv heard the faintest of tremors in her voice.

"When I was little … when I was no more than a small child, I remember an old lady, Ingrid, that my parents used to leave me with, to babysit. We were too little for school and there was no nursery, not up here in the mountains, so she would look after the children, four or five of us at a time. One day, one of the other children ran away, into the forest. When Ingrid found the boy, she sat us all down and told us a story. About things that lived in the woods, that slept out there, that waited. Things that only came out at night. Just a story, but the look in her eyes … I've never forgotten it. That old lady's words … I've heard them all night long."

She seemed to come back to herself and fell abruptly silent.

Malachi stared across at Hanna. There was a glimmer of hope in his voice.

"Whatever they are … maybe they've gone now … now it's not night. Maybe they were hungry. And now they took the others they're not."

Hanna stood and placed her fingers on the steel door handle.

"We'll see. Either way, we can't stay here any more. We need to look at the injured girl's ankle. We're all hungry, cold. And I'm pretty sure I'm not the only one that needs the toilet. We have to move."

Chapter Thirteen

They emerged into the daylight like zombies.

Gathered by the others in the lobby of the hostel, Tara shielded her eyes against the weak glow from the skylight and looked around at the rest of the group. There were only nine of them left. There had been at least thirty of them on the coach when they had first arrived at the bottom of the valley, maybe more.

And now there were just nine.

It was like a nightmare, a terrifying hallucination that had stretched on into the daylight and was impossible to wake up from. Apart from Ryan, it looked as if none of Tara's friends had survived the night. She wiped at her eyes and then tried to smile as Ryan squeezed her hand. At least he was still with her. Two of his teammates were with them too, Malachi and Jordan, and they stood on either side of Poppy like sentries, supporting her while she held her savaged ankle just above the floorboards.

Tara found she couldn't really bear to look at the wound too much. Poppy's face was white with pain, and Tara was glad that it hadn't been *her* ankle that had been too close to the underside of the minibus. She watched as Shiv kneeled down by Poppy and used a tatty jumper to try to bind Poppy's wound. Shiv had been friends with Ryan since they were little, and Tara knew that Shiv trained in the gym with the boys. Tara always felt a little judged by the other girl, as if Shiv reckoned that Ryan was too good for her, but they'd barely spoken before this trip.

Shiv stood up and took Ellie's hand in her own. Tara had chatted to Ellie once when they'd found themselves sat together in an assembly, but she wasn't from the right part of town for Tara and her to be friends. Her long blond hair was stringy, and her fingers were covered with cheap, showy gold rings. Ellie had told Tara once that she wanted to get into fashion, but Tara thought that Ellie's first move might be to take a long, hard look in the mirror.

Then there was the new boy, Charlie. Tara thought he looked a little bit like somebody that had just staggered out of a rock concert, with his scruffy dark hair that always seemed to be jutting out at jagged angles. Worse still, he dressed like a tramp, in an awful combination of hoodies and torn jeans. And bearing in mind the stories about him, and the fact that the police had bundled him out of school on more than one occasion, he certainly wasn't somebody that Tara wanted to be trapped alone with.

The German girl, though, was the one that Tara really couldn't stand. Or was she Austrian? Tara didn't think it mattered too much. Austrian or German, she was still a grade-A bitch. She might have helped them escape, but that didn't mean she could talk to them like crap or order them around. It was a shame, thought Tara, that it hadn't been Hanna that had been eaten first instead of Stefan, who had always been charming and polite. She wouldn't have minded being trapped alone with him.

While the rest of them waited, Hanna listened at the hostel door. Once she was satisfied that there was no noise other than the storm, she led them outside.

Ryan took Tara by the hand and gently pulled

her into the grey light. It was still snowing. In fact, Tara thought that the snow and wind might have been worse than ever. Her teeth chattered and she wrapped herself deeper into the folds of the old sleeping bag that Ryan had given to her, and that she now wore like a blanket.

For a while, the group huddled near to the safety of the hostel, looking this way and that, making sure that the streets really were deserted. Once Hanna was happy that they were on their own, she pointed over at the ski shop that they had crashed into the night before and the rest of the group trudged after her.

Tara didn't like Hanna and she certainly didn't trust her, with her threats and orders. She considered sowing the seeds of mutiny, but a far more pressing need to get out of the cold kept her jaw clamped shut.

As they walked, Hanna kept her metal hockey stick in one hand, the battered tip covered in dried, darkened blood. Malachi and Jordan were half-carrying Poppy, and every few steps her foot caught on the drifts of snow, eliciting a cry of pain from her lips. She had been sobbing for most of the night, so much so that Tara was pretty sure none of them had been able to sleep.

After a few minutes of trudging through the deepening snow, they reached the site of the crash the night before. Rather than go in through the back of the shop, Hanna took them round to the side, where the brick wall was interrupted by the front half of the minibus. She paused and looked back at the group, lingering for a moment on Ryan, who was still dressed in a shrunken hoodie and joggers. He shivered and trembled next to Tara, his hands stuffed into his pockets.

"Get yourselves coats, gloves, trousers, whatever you need, but be quick. Hypothermia will kill you just as surely as anything else if you don't get warm, but I don't want us staying out in the open for too long. Move quickly. Once you're ready, we'll get food for the little princess and any others of you that are hungry."

Tara scowled at her through the falling snow. "Do you mean me?"

Hanna ignored her question. Poppy rested her head on Jordan's shoulder and stared fearfully into the gloom of the shop.

"What if that thing … what if it's still in there?"

Hanna sighed, looked towards the shattered interior of the shop then raised her hockey stick. "Wait here."

She slipped into a space between the side of the minibus and the broken wall and vanished from view.

"I hope she gets eaten," hissed Tara. She nestled in closer to Ryan and felt him start to pull away. Tara realized that what she had been thinking had actually slipped out of her mouth, and she glanced up at Ryan.

"I didn't mean it. I'm scared. And I'm sick of being bossed around."

Ryan nodded dubiously and Tara glanced around the tiny village street. Now that it was daylight, now that they were out in the open, the night before felt even more like a dream. But she only had to look at Poppy's mauled ankle to know it had been real.

There was a noise from inside the shop, a gasping and hissing. Then there was a series of heavy thuds, one after another.

Shiv's dark eyes widened, and she took a step backwards. "Jesus, what is that? Do you think…?"

Hanna's head popped round the side of the wall and she eased her way out into the storm. "It's clear. If you want to get warm, you need to get moving."

Ellie stood stock still. "What was that noise?"

Hanna glanced down at the hockey stick by her side. Tara noticed that fresh blood dripped from the end of the metal on to the drifts of snow.

"You don't want to know. Trust me. Now get moving."

Chapter Fourteen

"I'm going to get down the mountain. I'm going to make a break for it."

Hanna processed Ryan's words while she tried to block out how the end of her hockey stick had become such a grisly mess. She looked the stocky rugby player up and down, considering his usefulness, and decided that he was one of the few potentially valuable members of the group.

"You'll never make it. Not in this storm. Not with the visibility as it is. Out there in the open you'll freeze to death in less than an hour. It's suicide."

Ryan held the skis in front of his chest defensively, a pair of poles tucked under his arm. "I'd rather take my chances on the mountain than up here, with those things. And if I get down there, I can get help. I can raise the alarm, get a rescue party up here."

Tara shook her head in disbelief. "You … you're not going to leave us, are you? You can't."

Hanna ran a hand through her hair, pushing her fringe out of her eyes. "The little princess is right. You can't. You've been skiing for what, a week? I wouldn't even consider it myself and I've been on the mountains since I was a baby."

Ryan shook his head and zipped up the padded jacket he'd found on a rack. "I skied down to the valley a few days ago. It wasn't that hard. Fast in places, sure, but I can handle it."

Hanna felt her eyes rolling in exasperation. "Since the day you slipped and slid on your way down to the valley there's been at least a metre of fresh powder. Nobody's been out there to piste it, to make it rideable. You've never skied in powder. It's not the same. And the chances of avalanche at the moment will be astronomical, not to mention getting lost or freezing to death."

Ryan ignored her, sat down and started to clip into a pair of ski boots he'd found. "Stefan said I had tons of natural ability. He said I was the best beginner skier he'd ever seen. I think I can make it."

Tara shook her head desperately. "Stefan didn't know everything. You ... you can't listen to what he said. He was friends with *her*, for God's sake."

Hanna fought back an angry response and gave the other girl a withering look. She'd had Tara's number the day she'd first seen the school party stumbling off the coach, with her expensive Burberry luggage, her perfect hair and nails, the haughty demeanour that stank of privilege and condescension. And maybe the teachers hadn't noticed it, but Hanna had seen the way Ryan looked at Tara, the way his eyes lit up when they fell on her.

Yes, Hanna had met dozens of people just like Tara before, striding around the mountain like they owned it.

And the worst thing was that Tara had everything Hanna wanted. Friends. Belonging. A boyfriend. A life.

Everything she'd turned her back on when she'd found herself dragged back to the desolate resort by some unfathomable yearning for answers.

Hanna took a moment to calm herself before she spoke again. "It's suicide to try to get down the mountain. It's minus ten out there, at least. Visibility's nothing. This storm won't last forever. But if that's what you want to do, then it's up to you, I'm not going to waste my time trying to talk sense into you."

Malachi grabbed a pair of boots off the rack and nodded. "Screw it. I've skied before. I'm with you. And I'd rather freeze than have one of those things grab me and drag me into the snow and do God knows what with me."

Shiv nodded. "Me too. Let's do it. Let's all do it." She grabbed a pair of skis off a nearby rack and took down a set of goggles.

Hanna watched Charlie take a pair of snowboard boots off the shelf, slip them on, then move a step closer to Ryan. There was something about the dark-eyed boy, something she couldn't quite put her finger on.

But out of all of them, he was the only one that Hanna felt a flicker of compassion towards.

Or saw as anything more than a chip to be gambled as she tried to make sense of all that was unfolding.

"She knows what she's saying, Ryan. She knows the mountain. You really want to die out there?"

Jordan glared in Charlie's direction. "What do you know, Mr Crim?"

Ryan waved Jordan's words away with a gloved hand and turned back to Charlie. "I've seen you snowboard. You're amazing. You should be coming too, not trying to talk us out of it." He looked up from where he was sitting and glanced around the group, his eyes blue and bright in his chiselled face. "You should all come. We'll be quick! We'll make it!"

Jordan shook his head and looked mournfully at the captain. "I can't ski for shit. What am I going to do? Run after you?"

Ellie wiped at her nose with the back of her hand. "Neither can I. And she definitely can't."

Hanna followed Ellie's gaze to Poppy, who was slouched down in a chair in the corner, blood starting to seep through the rough bandages that Shiv had applied.

Tara nodded firmly. "I can't ski either, or at least not very well. You're not going to leave *me*, are you?"

Hanna felt a perverse sense of satisfaction when Ryan barely wavered.

"I'll make it. We'll get help. It'll be OK, baby, I promise."

Tara's eyes started to brim with tears.

A few minutes was all it took for the three of them to fasten their boots and get themselves kitted out with goggles and helmets and a succession of layers. Hanna didn't bother to try to stop them, the gears in her mind still struggling to process exactly what had happened the night before.

Whatever she had expected from Matthias's garbled warning, it wasn't this.

Outside, the storm continued to scream and howl, the clothes on the racks rattling to and fro in the wind that whipped into the shop.

Tara called to Ryan imploringly one last time. "Please, Ryan, please. Don't leave me."

He glanced down at her through orange-tinted goggles and smiled. "I'll come back for you. I promise. Before it even gets dark, we'll be back."

He lifted his scarf up over his mouth and started towards the street beyond.

Hanna found herself calling his name before she could stop herself. "Ryan. Wait."

"If you're trying to talk us out of it—"

"I'm not. If you want to go, it's up to you. But take the blue, up by the lifts. It turns into a red after half a mile, then a black. That's the bit you need to watch. That's the bit that's going to be loaded with snow. That's where you need to take care. And don't stop or you'll freeze to death out there."

Ryan nodded. "Thanks."

He stared in Charlie's direction. "You coming?"

Hanna felt an odder flicker of relief when he shook his head slowly. "No. You go. Try and make it. Get help."

Ryan gestured towards the others, and the three of them picked up their skis and poles and started to clump towards the lifts, their heavy snow boots making their progress slow and laborious.

Hanna stood at the door and watched them go, wondering what would get to them first – the cold, the deadly pistes or the creatures. It was less than a minute before the storm swallowed them up, their fading footprints the only evidence that they had ever been there at all.

Chapter Fifteen

"Why didn't you go with them?"

Charlie ignored the question and took another bite of his Mars bar. Now that there was food, he suddenly realized how hungry he had been. He hadn't eaten since lunchtime the day before and his stomach growled at the sudden presence of food. He reached out and unwrapped another chocolate bar, a Snickers this time, and found Tara still staring at him.

He glanced around at the empty chairs and tables and shrugged. "I don't know. It wasn't because I particularly like any of you, that's for sure. I just didn't want to leave everyone up here."

Tara eyed him suspiciously then poured herself a glass of milk from a bottle inside the fridge. Despite the lack of power, the contents of the café's refrigerator were still fresh.

"But you … you'd be the last person I'd expect to

stay. After the things you must have done, you'd be the last person I'd expect to care about anyone other than yourself."

Charlie stared at her for a moment, considered a range of possible responses, then decided none of them would make things any better.

After Ryan and the others had faded like ghosts on the road out of the village, Hanna had brought the rest of them to this small café a few doors down from the Panoramic Hotel.

Charlie knew the place. Stefan had taken the group there for cake on the second day. There hadn't been many customers then, just the students from Charlie's school and one or two other hikers, but all the same the owner had been flustered and hassled, something Stefan had remarked on as being strangely out of character.

Today, no one had looked towards the Panoramic as they walked to the shop, and Charlie had been more than relieved when Hanna had tried the café door and found it unlocked. The last thing he had wanted to do was stand out in the open and revisit what had happened the night before. In the frosty air of the café, those that hadn't left with Ryan slumped in chairs around the room and salvaged what they could from behind the counter. Poppy sat in the corner, her wounded leg propped up on a chair, while Ellie and Jordan stared at the wall.

Hanna stood by the window, watching the falling snow through a tiny crack in the blinds. She had locked the front door behind them and dropped the blinds, but all the same Charlie felt far from safe. After a while, Hanna walked away from the window, stared at the counter and its empty glass cabinets then parked herself down next to Charlie and Tara. Her silver nose-ring caught the dim light that sneaked in from outside, and she had a cup in one hand, a half-eaten pastry in the other. She glanced back at the storm then shook her head dismissively. "They shouldn't have gone. They'll never make it."

Tara stared at Hanna bitterly. "If I could ski, I'd have gone, too. I wish I could have gone. Better that than being stuck up here with those things and you."

Hanna took a sip from her cup of milk. "Well, don't let me stop you from joining them. It would certainly make my life a little more pleasant without you tagging along like a lost little puppy, bitching and whining."

She took another mouthful of her milk then looked up at Charlie, her grey eyes boring into him. "So. I've seen you snowboard, and you know what you're doing. And it doesn't look like you're the most popular student here. I know you're not scared of getting caught in an avalanche out there. So why didn't you go?"

Charlie shifted uneasily and scrunched up the wrapper from his chocolate bar. Hanna's piercing gaze never left him, and he realized he wasn't going to get away without giving an answer. He shrugged and looked back at her.

"My dad was a lifeguard. Well, he was a lot of things, but he was a lifeguard when he was older. And he always said that you should do whatever you can to help others. Selfless, I think he said. You should be selfless. I think its pretty fair to say I haven't exactly followed in his footsteps. But this morning, when Ryan and the others were leaving, I couldn't get my dad's words out of my head."

Tara snorted. "Oh, so suddenly you're all about helping others? Didn't sound that way from what

I heard the receptionists saying back at school. Or when the police came in to mop you up."

A gust of wind made the door rattle and Tara shook her head ruefully. "Sorry. I didn't mean that. I just can't believe he went. I can't believe Ryan left me. I mean, what if those things get in here? Who's going to protect me now he's gone?"

Hanna shot her a dismissive look. "Not me. That's for sure."

Charlie tried to slide between the two girls before their relationship deteriorated any further. "Those things have gone, whatever they were. You'd hear them if they were still here. You'd see them."

Tara swore, stood up abruptly and stalked off to sit by the others at the furthest table from the door. Both Jordan and Poppy were looking lost and desolate, Ellie trying and failing to comfort them. Out of the corner of his eye, Charlie watched Tara lean in towards the others, her fingers gesturing in Hanna's direction. He suspected that whatever she was saying was far from pleasant.

With Tara out of earshot, he glanced back up at Hanna. "What did you find in there, in the shop?"

Hanna stared at her drink for a moment then

looked back up at Charlie. "That thing. The one that took a chunk out of Poppy. It was pinned under the wheels of the minibus last night. And when I went in there today, it was still there. Still moving."

She took another sip of her drink, and seemed to suppress a shiver. "So I stopped it moving."

When Charlie spoke again, his voice was barely a whisper. "What the hell happened last night? What are they?"

Hanna took a deep breath. "I don't know. That thing under the wheels of the bus, whatever it was, it didn't look … normal. Or maybe I imagined it. It was dark in there."

Hanna shuddered. "Part of me thinks we should have made a break for it, like the others. But I know we wouldn't have made it."

Charlie studied her, the gears in his mind rolling and shifting. "You know something, don't you? Something you're not telling us?"

Hanna shook her head quickly. "I'm just as scared and confused as you. And if I knew anything, I'd have told you."

There was something in Hanna's eyes that suggested otherwise. "So what do we do?"

Hanna glanced towards the doors, then over at the shadow of the Panoramic Hotel. "We need to keep out of sight, in case those things are still here. We need to make sure they don't know where we are. Yesterday, when Stefan and I were looking for the villagers, I felt like I was being watched. But only on the edge of town, not here, not in the centre. And I trust my instincts. So we need to make sure that when it gets dark, if those things come out again, they don't know where we're hiding. It won't be long until help comes. A day, maybe two. Particularly as the people in the valley can't get hold of us. We just need to stay out of sight long enough for the storm to clear."

Chapter Sixteen

On paper, the scenario was like a dream.

Trapped for endless hours, alone in the dark with a pretty girl who couldn't bear to be more than an inch away from him, her arms wrapped around him. The problem was that Nico himself was terrified and he had no idea what to do next. That, and the fact that at some point during what had happened he'd wet his pants.

After those things had smashed into the hotel, after they had dragged Chris and Jacob and Sarah and God knew who else away into the storm, the world had turned into a nightmare.

Nico had seen some of the survivors sprinting up to the first floor and a few more fleeing along the corridors downstairs. More by accident than anything, he had found himself pushed along out of the lobby in a tide of screaming, frantic students.

Then he'd taken an elbow to the face, fallen,

slipped and tumbled down a set of stairs that led to the basement. Luckily for him, it had only been four stairs down to a small corridor at the bottom. Unaware, uncaring or maybe both, the other students had raced on, perhaps heading for the back of the hotel and the fire escape there.

Nico had staggered to his feet, rubbed at his ear and glanced around. He hadn't been on his own. Two tearful brown eyes had stared imploringly at him out of the gloom.

"Please! Please, help me, help me get away, please!"

For a few seconds he'd stared at Leandra, unsure of a way forwards. He'd often imagined himself as the hero of an action or sci-fi film, but when he'd finally found himself in the role, he had wanted to be anywhere else on earth.

With a whimper, he'd led Leandra down the corridor to the ski storage room at the end of the hall.

Back on the first day of the trip, Nico had managed to break the tip off one of his skis, and the hotel manager had burned some strange, smelly resin on to the crack to try to fix it. The ski room was small, musty and cold, but it had a heavy metal door at one end and a rack, which could be slid over to block the only way in. He'd herded Leandra into the room, slammed the door shut, blocked it and then had started to pray.

To his disbelief, it had worked. Nothing had stalked down the corridor to investigate their tiny hiding place. He and Leandra had shuffled as far away from the rack as they could, huddled under a pile of old ski jackets that they had found in a corner, and sat together in the dark.

The first hour had been the worst. From somewhere above where Nico and Leandra shivered and sobbed had come the shouts and howls of the things that had taken Stefan.

Then there had been another noise. A student in the corridor above, crying and pleading. Nico had felt his blood run cold when, a few moments later, one of the intruders heard the survivor outside and came for him.

Once that happened, Nico had to jam his hands to his ears and bow his head down by Leandra's, whimpering to himself and begging for the awful wet noises to stop.

As he had sat there, trying not to hear the sounds but picking up every tiny detail, his mind had kept going back to what he had seen earlier. The face of one of the things as it burst in through the glass and pounced on one of the few girls that had ever lowered herself to talk to Nico.

Its skin was pale and wrinkled, its eyes clear and translucent. But it had been the mouth that haunted Nico most of all: its jaws wide and vicious and filled with misshapen, jagged, dirty fangs that protruded irregularly, like stalactites on the ceiling of a cave. The image had jumped back and forth in his mind, over and over, a visual accompaniment to the awful slurping and sucking from just outside the door. He was pretty sure that it had been then that his bladder had let go, soaking him.

Some time later he must have fallen asleep, Leandra moaning and jerking next to him. When she finally woke him from thin, terrified dreams, they had no idea what time it was, day or night. The only thing they were sure of was that apart from the howl of the wind, the world above was silent.

And then they heard the voices.

Chapter Seventeen

"Why did you bring us here? What's wrong with you?"

Hanna ignored Tara's words and paced around the ravaged dining room, as if she were trying to find some clue within the chaos. The tattered curtains billowed and whipped in the wind, and the shards of glass on the floor glittered in the faint daylight.

For once, Charlie found himself feeling the same way as Tara. Every gust of wind made him jump and he found himself constantly fighting an urge to run for the door. When Hanna had first revealed her plan to return to the hotel he had tried his best to talk her out of it, but she had been adamant. Tara had tried to recruit Ellie and Jordan in a takeover bid for leadership, but Hanna had seemed happy enough to go off on her own. She'd wanted to see the hotel in the daylight, and she had been bent on finding out if the destruction from the night before might reveal any more about their attackers.

And there had been no talking her out of it.

Unwilling to lose their resourceful guide, the rest of the survivors had trailed Hanna the few metres through the relentless blizzard towards the Panoramic Hotel. Fresh snow had hidden any signs of the bloodshed from the night before, but even so Charlie's mind kept picturing the horrors that might be lying underneath the deep drifts, the things he had seen when he had hunched shivering on the rooftop above.

At first Tara had refused to go in at all. It was only when she'd realized that she would be left outside on her own that she sighed loudly and reluctantly padded into the hotel behind Jordan and Poppy.

The door swung to and fro in the harsh wind, the few shards of glass that still clung on to the frame flecked with blood. Charlie wondered if some of it was Stefan's. A plastic chair had been overturned in the lobby, and the old computer that had manned the hotel desk now lay discarded on the ground, its cracked screen reflecting the blizzard outside.

While Hanna stalked from spot to spot, the rest of them tried their best to step over the patches of blood on the floor. One large slick led away into the dining room. Jordan let out a choked sob and turned away from the sight, but Hanna stared at it wordlessly then followed it. Charlie chewed at his lip for a moment then went after her.

The dining room was like something out of a nightmare. Dark stains spattered the carpet and sofas. Glass and torn shreds of curtain and clothes covered the floor. But of the students that had once sat in the ravaged chairs, there was no sign at all.

Charlie wanted to get out as quickly as he could, and he scanned his surroundings, trying to avert his eyes from the chair in the corner where Kelsey had been sitting when it had all started. The brown leather of the old sofa was stained as if by oil, black patches leading away in a trail, like footprints on a ghastly treasure map.

He stole one more glance at the chair, felt a wave of vomit at the back of his throat and stumbled out into the lobby.

While Ellie stood by the door with her hood up, Poppy watched Charlie from where she sat over behind the reception desk, her mauled leg propped up on a bin by her feet. Charlie pulled the jacket he had taken from the ski shop closer around his ears and moved over to sit on the desk next to her.

"How's your ankle?"

There were dark lines under Poppy's eyes, and beads of sweat stood out on her forehead. She drew in a jagged breath and looked up at him. "It hurts like hell. Like I've been bitten by a dog or something."

She paused, wiped at her eyes and shifted her leg on the bin. "I need something for the pain, just to make the throbbing less. Could you do something for me? Could you see what you can find?"

Charlie nodded and dug around in the drawers next to where she sat. There was a first-aid box in the second drawer, and it didn't take Charlie long to find a pack of painkillers. He handed two to Poppy. She took them gratefully, dry swallowed them and motioned for two more. Charlie stared at her, shrugged and gave her what she wanted.

For a moment neither of them spoke, and then Poppy sighed and looked up at Charlie. "I'm sorry. You're not what I thought you were, you know. So I'm sorry."

Charlie shrugged. "For what? You never did

anything to me."

Poppy wiped at her eyes. "Yeah, I did. I was in that English class with you. I've got a lot of friends. I could have made things easier for you, not ostracized you. Not whispered rumours and gossip about you whenever they dragged you away to the office. I didn't know what was going on with you. And maybe I should have asked."

Charlie looked down at her and shook his head. "Forget it. I heard the stories about me, too. I read some of them on the wall in the sixth-form toilets. Not all of them were lies. And maybe I could have done with a little help. But that school never seemed like the friendliest place to me. Neither did the other kids there."

Poppy brushed a rogue strand of curly auburn hair from her face and winced at a fresh spasm of pain. "Do you think we'll ever see the school again? Do you think we'll get away from here?"

Before Charlie could answer, Jordan hurried into the lobby. He had been by one of the corridors that led to the back of the hotel. Ellie was still standing by the door, unwilling to commit to fully entering the lobby, and at the tone in Jordan's voice she took a step backwards into the storm outside.

"There's something. Back there, down some stairs just along the corridor. I swear it, I heard a noise."

Hanna stalked in from the dining room, the metal hockey stick held in both her hands. "What noise?"

Jordan shook his head, his tight blond curls dancing in front of his eyes. "I dunno. Crying, I think – voices, too. I'm not imagining it, though. I heard something, for sure. Then when I crept closer it stopped. Like it heard me."

Hanna looked past him, down the corridor that disappeared into shadow.

"Show me."

Jordan nodded reluctantly and started to go back the way he had come. Charlie's heart was pounding in his chest, his legs shaky, but all the same he found himself rising from the desk and slowly walking after the others. As he went, he noticed a shattered glass panel on the wall, a fire axe suspended inside it. Gently, he unclipped the axe, tested its weight then continued after Hanna.

Jordan had paused halfway down the corridor, at a place where a puddle of dried blood seemed to almost point towards a small set of stairs, going down to a basement level. He was careful not to stand in the blood, his whispers bouncing off the linoleum of the floor as he nodded down the corridor.

"There. It was down there. I don't know, but I think that whatever it was heard my footsteps and tried to be quiet. Maybe … maybe it was one of those things."

Hanna licked her lips then carefully descended the stairs. Charlie glanced at Jordan, but the other boy shook his head.

"Fill your boots, Crim. I ain't going near that door."

Charlie moved away to where Hanna had stopped, her head to one side. Her words were directed at the looming door, her accent more jagged than usual. "Hallo. Is somebody there? If you are, you need to show yourself. *Now.*"

Noises came from the other side of the door and Charlie took an involuntary step backwards, his hands tight around the handle of the axe. A low screech echoed down the corridor, something heavy being slid to one side. Then the door opened a crack and a face peered through the gap.

"Thank God. Please tell me you've brought help.

Please tell me those things are gone."

Hanna lowered her hockey stick then shook her head slowly from side to side.

Chapter Eighteen

"You're sure this old hostel is safe? It feels like a tomb, like no one's stepped inside here for decades. It's creepy."

The girl called Hanna glanced up from the contents of the can she was eating from and fixed Nico with a steely glare.

"You have a better idea? An underground bunker somewhere, maybe, or a vault in some bank I don't know about hidden in the village?"

Nico shook his head penitently. Hanna's grey eyes bored into him for a moment longer. Her face had a hard, scary quality that made Nico want to avoid getting on the wrong side of her.

"You don't? Then the answer to your question is *no*, I don't think this place is safe. But I don't have a better idea. It's nearly twilight, and I don't think any of us want to go out and try to find somewhere more secure, particularly if those things come out again once it gets dark. I don't think anywhere is safe. But this is the best we've got for now."

Thankfully, Hanna looked away and went back to the food in the tin. Nico wasn't sure what it was she was eating, but it stank. He started to remark on the fact, but decided it would be unwise.

Next to him Tara leaned forwards and, in an antagonistic tone, said: "I told you we should have gone with Ryan. Even if we couldn't ski, we could still have walked. Anything is better than this. I mean, what are we going to do if those things do come out? It's going to be dark soon."

Hanna swore in German, put her tin and fork to one side, and gave Tara an icy stare. "You would have frozen to death in an hour. Not that it would have been a great loss. And what are we going to do? Well, we could put on some lights, play a little music, have a drink, maybe even get a board game out."

She took a deep breath and tucked a stray strand of hair behind one ear. "We're going to hide. The windows are boarded up, the only doors to the outside are bolted, and this lantern is the only sign we're here, apart from your whining. Soon we'll put out the light, climb under our blankets, and pray those things from last night don't know we're here. But there's still time for you to join your little boyfriend. Although I don't want to think about the state you might find him in."

Tara shook her head, glancing at Ellie and Jordan for a glimmer of solidarity. "Better than here. With you. You two agree with me, don't you? We should have gone, shouldn't we? With Ryan, out into the storm, rather than staying here. Anyway, he's probably down in the valley by now. Safe. We'll see who's right when he comes back up here, to rescue us. We'll see how clever you are then."

Hanna sat up and leaned forwards. She picked up her fork and held the pointed end at Tara. Tara slowly slid backwards into her sleeping bag at the threat.

"Another word. Just one more word."

Across from Hanna, Leandra pulled the blanket closer around her shoulders and studied the Austrian girl. "Who put you in charge? I mean, no offence, but I don't know you. None of us know you. How do you know what's best?"

Hanna stared at Leandra for a moment before

she replied. "I don't. I'm making this up as I go along. And as I said to your friend Tara, if you don't like it, you know where the door is. I'd be happier on my own."

The atmosphere in the musty lounge had become more than a little uncomfortable, and Nico concentrated on his food to avoid the brewing conflict, forcing another mouthful of his cold ravioli. There hadn't been much choice in the small convenience store that Hanna had hurriedly looted on the way back to the boarded-up hostel, and the canned food that Nico had chosen was even worse cold than it would have been warmed up. Even though he was starving he still couldn't stomach it, and he found himself putting his can down on the dusty floorboards.

Across from him, Charlie stared up at the boarded-up windows and Nico followed his gaze. Earlier, Charlie had explained how Hanna knew about the old hostel, and even though Nico's childhood had been the very opposite of joyful, he still had to wonder about the type of adolescence where children spent their time wandering around in old, dilapidated relics. The aged hostel was creepy with a capital 'C', and Nico was relieved when Hanna clicked off the lantern. At least then he didn't have to look at the awful Gothic oil-painted scenes on the walls and the cobwebs that were draped over them.

"You think they'll come out again tonight? You think they'll try to find us?"

The words were Leandra's. Nico might not have had much contact with her back home, but after a night trapped alone in the hotel basement with her he would know her voice anywhere.

"Maybe not," Charlie answered. "They didn't find us last night. And maybe they're gone. Maybe they got what they wanted."

Jordan seemed to come out of a daze and he glared across at Charlie. "How do you know so much? You an expert now? An expert on nothing but being a screw-up. Should be Jacob standing where you are, or Angus. Not a loser like you."

Jordan stumped off to the corner, pulled his sleeping bag up over his face, and fell silent. Charlie ignored him, his eyes never leaving the deserted streets.

Nico watched the thin silvery beams of light that

slid in through the cracks in the wooden shutters. They were fading by the second.

Someone yawned. From the sofa in the corner of the room came a low, stifled sobbing. Nico didn't know what had happened to Poppy's ankle, but it looked like she had stuck her leg through the bars of a shark cage and not pulled it back quite quickly enough. She wiped at her nose and spoke to no one in particular.

"They're out there, aren't they? They were watching us today, waiting."

Nico cleared his throat, and spoke with a certainty he didn't feel. "Maybe not. Maybe—"

A low, hungry moan rose above the howl of the wind, Jordan swore loudly in response, and Nico heard the words crumble and fade on his lips.

Chapter Nineteen

Hanna had been right.

It had been madness to go out into the storm.

They were lost, freezing, starving and exhausted. And the daylight was almost gone.

When they'd first left, Shiv had been filled with hope. The three of them had buzzed with a heady relief as the grey buildings of the village faded into the blizzard behind them. Kaldgellan was like an abattoir now, the stink of death all over it. And the thought that those things might come out again once it grew dark was too terrible to consider.

Shiv had jumped on board Ryan's plan without a second thought. The wind had been ferocious, the snow relentless and the drifts waist-deep in places, but she'd have taken the hellish conditions any day, rather than sitting in the village, waiting for the weak daylight to fade away.

For a while it had seemed makeable. Shiv could

more than keep up with the boys, and she had spent countless hours in the gym, training, rowing, squatting, sweating. She had little doubt that if it were a matter of strength and endurance, she would make it down to the valley. Ryan had taken Hanna's advice and followed what was once a gentle blue run. But now it was impossible to tell where the slope started and finished, and the snow had been far too deep to ride.

Shiv had skied before and she was competent, but all the same she couldn't make her way through the thick, cloying powder. And even if she could have done, she would still have had to wait for Ryan and Malachi, who barely made it a dozen metres before losing their skis and poles. In the end, they had started to wade through the snow, staggering onwards, trying to keep the descending slope in front of them.

It had been hopeless.

There was no way of knowing which direction they were headed in, other than downwards, and they couldn't see more than a few feet through the blizzard. The snow was chest-deep in places and at one point they had had to dig Malachi out from a huge drift that swallowed him up to his neck.

All the time, the wind tore at them, pushing them this way and that, and the cold gnawed into their bones. As they struggled on, Shiv slowly started to lose the feeling in her fingers and toes.

It felt like they had been walking for hours, barely making any ground, when Shiv stopped and turned back to them, her words torn away by the keening wind. They had chanced upon a lift hut, away at the side of the slope they clung to, and Shiv suggested they shelter there and get their breath back. As fit as she was, Shiv had been almost sobbing with fatigue. The others had been too tired to even reply.

The tiny lift station was locked, but Shiv used her skis to break the glass next to the door handle. The hut was cramped, little more than a wooden shed with a control panel and a chair in one corner, but it was out of the wind and the blizzard, and the three of them had slumped to the floor with exhaustion. Nobody had really bothered to speak, or to voice what Shiv supposed they had all been thinking. That Hanna had been right.

It was just as the light drained out of the sky that the noises found their way into the tiny hut. At first

Shiv told herself it was the howling of the wind. But as the light on the slopes outside slipped from blue to grey, Shiv found Ryan's eyes meeting her own.

They had been friends since primary school, never crossing the line into anything more, but Ryan was someone she always turned to, always sought out when she needed a confidant.

When Ryan's mum and dad had split up when he was eight, before his move to the flats, they had sat in the den up in the tree at the back of his garden and talked about whatever they could think of to block the shouting and screaming from the other side of his parents' patio windows. And when Luke had dumped Shiv last year, it had been Ryan who had taken her down to the waterfront for a beer and a chat, and Ryan who had reassured her that she was better off without him. In all they'd been through, she had never seen him scared before. And she'd never heard fear in his voice. Until now.

"That noise is getting closer. We can't stay here. Shit!"

Shiv nodded and kicked Malachi awake from where he was curled up on the floor of the hut. His eyes looked delirious, exhausted, and when another howl echoed in the twilight his face looked as if it might crumble and break.

The three of them scrambled outside. It was as if someone had turned the storm up to an even fiercer setting and the wind almost knocked Shiv flat on to her face. She helped Malachi to stay upright, and her eyes caught a glimpse of movement at the top of the slope above their heads.

Shapes.

Figures.

Coming closer.

Shiv heard herself screaming. Somehow she couldn't stop. When she turned towards Ryan, her voice no longer sounded like her own.

"Jesus, they're here, they're coming for us, we need to move, now!"

Chapter Twenty

Charlie sat by the window, peering out at the wintry scene below through the tiniest crack in the shutters. Between the raging blizzard and the faintest glimmer of light from the moon, it was hard to make out much at all. But although he could hear shrieks and howls on the wind, there was no sign of movement on the street below.

It was cold in the hostel, so cold that his breath hung around his face, still and unmoving. He slid down from the window, zipped up his sleeping bag a little higher then wriggled across so that he was next to the small huddle of figures that lay on the wooden floorboards. A rumble of wind seemed to rock the building and one of the group swore quietly. Charlie saw a vague movement as the figure lying nearest to him turned in his direction.

"Anything out there?"

Charlie just made out Leandra's profile in the

gloom, her long black hair and the dark hollow of her eyes. The words were barely a whisper.

"No. Nothing. I can hear them out there, somewhere nearby. But I can't see anything moving except the snow."

Leandra slid closer to him in her sleeping bag, so that her shoulder almost touched his. "I'm scared. I can't stop shaking. What time do you think it is?"

Charlie shrugged. "One a.m., maybe two."

It felt as if a chasm separated them from the dawn. Leandra sighed quietly next to him. "Can we talk? I can't sleep, and I don't want to think about, about—"

Charlie cut her off before she could finish. "Yeah, if you want to. I don't want to lie here counting the minutes either."

Leandra moved an inch closer, her hair brushing Charlie's ear. "We were in English together, weren't we, and art? We never really talked, though, did we?"

Charlie didn't answer, his mind revisiting all the times when he'd needed somebody to talk to and nobody had been there. A longing screech echoed on the wind. Leandra shuddered next to him.

"I loved our art lessons. I could have sat in that classroom all day long. That's what I wanted to do with my life – be an artist, a painter. I'd give anything to be back there now."

Charlie pictured the small monochrome classroom, the dead afternoons spent watching the clock and doodling on the back page of his notebook while the teacher droned on to a uninterested, disaffected audience. It seemed a lifetime ago now.

Leandra breathed out through her nose. "What do you think's happening? What do you think those things are?"

Charlie chewed at a piece of chapped skin on his bottom lip. "I don't know. I really don't know."

The silence seemed to stretch on for minutes, hours. Somebody snored and coughed on the other side of the room. Leandra shuffled an inch closer to Charlie. "Can I tell you a secret? My friend, Fatima, the Muslim girl with the nose-ring, she had a thing for you. She told me she used to sit there and stare at you all lesson. You remember her? Pretty, short, used to sit at the back of the English class?"

Charlie shook his head slowly. "No. I mean, I

think I know who she was, but I had no idea…"

Leandra's head jiggled next to his as she nodded. "She knew you didn't. Still liked you, though. Said she didn't care about what people said about you, that you were a lot more interesting than text transformation."

Charlie didn't know what to say. He'd never even spoken to Fatima, and wouldn't have known what to say if he had.

Leandra turned her mouth closer to his ear. Her voice seemed to drop a little lower, her lips only a few inches from his skin. "Can I tell you something else?"

Charlie nodded. He was suddenly almost as anxious about Leandra's closeness to him as he was about the storm outside. His mouth felt dry when he replied. "If you want to."

Leandra was still, unmoving, seeming to weigh her words. "I was going to run away. I was going to get back from this trip, get home, pack as much crap as I could fit into my backpack, and I was going to go."

Charlie tried to pinpoint her wide eyes in the darkness. "Where? Why?"

Leandra rolled on to her side so that she faced him, and her fingers drifted up towards her face, twisting in her hair. "They were going to marry me off. My mum and dad. Had it all planned, the guy picked out. As soon as I hit nineteen, that was going to be it. But you know what…"

She fell silent for a moment, and Charlie thought she might be crying. She sniffed and shook her head.

"You know, I thought *screw you*. I'll do what I want. I'll run away, down to London, stay with friends there, find someone I love, not someone I'm told I'm going to be with, find—"

A low shriek rose with the storm outside and Charlie felt Leandra jump next to him, her words caught in her throat. She was quiet for a few seconds then she took a deep breath and spoke again, a little louder now.

"I told my dad once. Told him I didn't want to get married to someone he'd picked out. Told him I wanted to marry someone I loved, or at least someone I fancied, wanted to be with, you know. And you know what he said? He said God wanted me to marry Subith. And he was worried that if I didn't, I'd go to hell."

She fell quiet and Charlie started to wonder if she was going to speak again. He realized he wanted her to. Anything was better than just lying there, waiting to be discovered.

She swore quietly and sighed. "And I wonder if this … if he was right, and this is it. Hell."

"Bullshit."

Charlie jumped at the new voice that hissed in the darkness. Hanna sat up, clicked on the lantern then shielded it with her blanket so that it gave off only the faintest glimmer of light. Even so, Charlie could see the anger in her eyes.

"He was wrong, your father. There's no heaven, no hell. And to say that because you wouldn't do what he told you to? When you get back, you can tell him that."

Leandra stared towards the source of the words. "You believe that? That we'll make it home? I want to. I want to so much."

Charlie saw Hanna sit up in the twilight, her black hair sliding forwards into her eyes.

"Think about your life back home. Fix on it, fix on your hopes, on being that artist you wanted to be. Focus on whatever you can if it helps you to get through this."

Tara's voice came from somewhere down by Charlie's feet. "There was so much I wanted to do with my life."

Poppy groaned in her sleep somewhere in the darkness, muttering to herself. Leandra glanced in her direction then looked over at Tara.

"What did you want to be?"

Tara yawned and sat up. "Be? I didn't really want to *be* anything. I was going to travel around the world, ski in the mountains, walk along the beach in Thailand, safari in Africa. I was going to have such an amazing life. I shouldn't be here. This shouldn't have happened to me. None of it."

Hanna swore in German. "What a shame that the poor little rich girl didn't get to live her life of vacant blandness. *Scheisse.*"

Tara's whispered words were tinged with bile. "Rich enough so that I wouldn't have to work as some butch guide in the mountains, dying my hair black and shaving it half off and dressing like a man."

Hanna stared at Tara through the half-light.

"My hair's black naturally. And this *butch guide* is the reason you're still alive. The reason you're still bitching and whining and telling us about the ridiculous life you had planned. You know, I've met people like you before, dozens of people like you. My brother died because of people like you."

Tara sniffed. "You don't know anything about me."

Hanna snorted. "*Ja*, I do. I've spent the last two years showing idiots like you around the mountain, making sure that they don't get lost, fall off a cliff, freeze to death. Rich idiots that think they own the world, and that they can speak to the rest of us like crap. People that have it all. People just like you. You're all the same."

Tara shook her head, her eyes poking out from the top of her silver sleeping bag. "I'm not. Not any more. Maybe I was, once, but two years ago my dad lost his job, then he and my mum broke up and we had to sell two of our houses. We might even have to sell my mum's place in Switzerland, that's how bad it's got. That's why I came on the trip, because we couldn't go to Verbier this year. That's why I'm at our awful school instead of one of the private schools around Bristol. We haven't got any money, not any more. I wish it wasn't true. I wish we could get it back. But we can't."

Charlie watched as Hanna wound herself up again, but he leaned across in her direction and whispered her name before she could speak.

"Hanna, how did your brother die?"

Hanna glanced at him, the fire fading from her eyes, her face suddenly unsure. "Another time. If we make it through tonight I'll tell you."

Nico's head appeared over by Poppy, the bobbles on his orange hat shifting in the shadows. "What are they? I know you … I know Hanna doesn't want to talk about it, but what are those things? That's all I can think about. I can't sleep for wondering what the hell is going on. What are they? Where did they come from? Why is this happening?"

Hanna glanced in his direction. It looked to Charlie as if she wasn't going to answer, then she shook her head wearily. "The old folk in these mountains say they're haunted. Cursed. There was a story they told us, when we were little, before I moved away. About creatures, things that came out at night. But they were just the kind of stories lots of parents tell their children. Just *mull*, what would you English say, crap, a load of old fairy tales. I don't know what those things are. And what help would it be anyway?"

Charlie couldn't shake the odd sensation that Hanna knew more than she was letting on, but Nico continued to stare at her.

"But they ... they *ate* some of the others. I saw them. And they only seem to come out at night. And ... their teeth. Like ... like a shark's, but bigger, worse. I've seen *Dracula*, *Fright Night*, *Nosferatu*. They ... they're vampires, aren't they?"

While Tara rolled her eyes, Hanna fired an angry reply in Nico's direction. "There's no such thing as vampires! They're people! That's all they are, and something's happened to them, something's—"

Charlie sat up, held out his hand. "Can you hear that? There's someone out there, calling. Listen."

Chapter Twenty-one

Even with Nico's sight restricted by the tiny cracks in the shutter and the blinding force of the blizzard, there was no mistaking the figure that trudged through the snow below.

Nico had no idea where Chris had been for the past twenty-four hours, how he could have escaped, or where he could have hidden. But now his best friend was outside the hostel, staggering from door to door, desperately searching the neighbouring chalets for help.

Chris loved *Warcraft*, as much as if not more than Nico did. The two of them would sit there, side by side, or connected from their houses by headsets if it was late at night.

And now, as Nico watched Chris stagger like a drunkard into the force of the wind, he wanted to run down, shout to his friend, drag him in from the storm.

Instead he found he couldn't move.

In the virtual world they explored together, Nico had carried out all manner of heroic tasks, taken on any number of unholy monsters. Nocturnal demons had fled from the bite of his sword, wealthy lords and kings rewarding him for his exploits and skill.

But now, when things mattered, he was frozen to the spot, no better than the worst kind of coward.

Instead, it was Charlie who backed away from the shutters and turned towards the door. He held an axe in one hand, its red handle catching in the light of the lantern. Nico watched as Hanna's hand shot out and caught the sleeve of Charlie's jacket.

Her words were a snake's hiss in the darkness. "What the hell are you doing?"

Charlie tried to pull his arm away and found it held fast. "I'm going to go downstairs, open the door, let him in. We can't just leave him out there."

Next to Nico, Ellie put her hand over her mouth. "What if they … what if those things are out there? What if they see?"

Hanna nodded slowly. "She's right. There are seven of us up here. And there's one boy down there. There's a chance this might be a trap."

She looked from face to face, struggling to discern the reaction of her audience in the low light. "We need to see what they do, how they hunt. We need to find out all we can. And if we let him in, if they're watching, they might just kill us all. It's not a risk I'm prepared to take."

Her voice was cold, calculating, and even though it was his friend on the street below, Nico found himself more than thankful. But underpinning his relief was a strong tide of guilt, shame even. Nico's virtual alter ego would have gone after his friend in a heartbeat.

Charlie stared at Hanna, his voice a whisper. "I'm not sure it's up to you."

Nico moved away from the shutter and stepped between them. "Chris. His name's Chris. We've been friends since we were at pre-school. He's my best friend." He stared at the floor, unable to meet Charlie's eyes. "But I don't think we can let him in."

Charlie shook his head. "Well, I'm not going to just leave him out there."

Hanna let go of Charlie's sleeve. Nico noticed that she tightened her grip on the bloodied metal hockey stick in her other hand.

"Then we are going to have a serious disagreement."

Behind Nico, Jordan swore quietly. The tall youth had made his way to the window and he squinted down through the gaps in the shutters.

"Shit. There's something else further down the street, something… Oh shit, it's one of those things, it's one of—"

Hanna grabbed the front of Charlie's coat and pulled him to the floor. Then she slid up, to the crack of the shutters, a flicker of curiosity in her grey eyes. "Get down! All of you! And switch off that lantern. You can't help him now!"

Nico numbly slid down to his knees. A sound rose above the storm. A voice. First begging, then screaming.

Soon there was just the wind.

Hanna still kneeled by the boarded-up windows, her eyes level with the first of the cracks.

Nico peered at her from where he shivered on his knees. She had the look of a hunter, someone watching the movements of their prey before they prepared to lift their rifle and take a shot. Something about her curious demeanour made Nico wonder what else Hanna knew, and if there were things she wasn't willing to share with the other survivors.

After a while she glanced at him, shook her head slowly from side to side and slid down to join the others on the floor.

"Everybody get as far away from the window as you can. And if you want to last the night, don't make a sound."

Chapter Twenty-two

Shiv wanted to die.

She had lost the feeling in her fingers and toes hours earlier, and now her nose and the rest of her face felt lifeless and numb. Hanna had told them that they'd be dead in less than an hour out in the storm without shelter.

But she had been wrong, on that count if nothing else.

Shiv had frostbite, for sure, and if somebody was to miraculously turn up now and rescue her out of the blue she was pretty certain that she'd be living out the rest of her days with no fingers, no toes and just a gap where her nose had been.

But she wasn't dead, not yet.

Something kept Shiv alive. It might have been the sight of the figures that crept and danced in the blizzard just an arm's length away from her, jagged teeth clamping open and shut convulsively.

Or maybe it was Ryan.

Just beyond the figures, Ryan's clear blue eyes stared glassily at her. The thing that had killed him crouched on his chest, a clutch of flesh and entrails dangling like spaghetti from its mouth, a slick of blood down its chin. Its dark eyes slid towards Shiv as it ate, pupils swimming with hunger and hatred.

At the hotel, Shiv hadn't really caught a glimpse of the creatures that had crashed through the windows and taken her friends, not up close. She had caught flickers, shapes, but without her glasses they had been blurred, indistinct. Now, by the sliver of moonlight that fought its way through the clouds and snow, she saw it all.

When they had first heard the howls in the cramped confines of the lift station, Shiv and the others had made a desperate break for it. They hadn't got far. Malachi had been barely a dozen metres from the door of the lift hut before he'd tumbled over into the deep snow.

And then they were on him.

Shiv had chanced a quick look back, and seen Malachi on his front in the snow, a thin, pale-faced figure pinning him down. Curled, dirty fingernails were reaching for his neck. Malachi hadn't even had time to beg.

Ryan and Shiv had made it a little further. Shiv had been panting, Ryan swearing, both of them committed to getting down the mountain and as far away from the lift station as they could.

They'd both fallen around the same time, their skis sinking into the snow and their bodies tumbling down the slope with the momentum of their descent. The only difference had been that Shiv had slid and rolled a little bit further than Ryan. And that had been what had saved her.

She had heard a loud crack as a hidden rock brought her to a sudden halt, and then a heartbeat later she had felt a massive jolt of pain in her lower leg. After that she'd passed out.

It was minutes later when she had woken up. She knew it hadn't been long because Ryan had still been breathing as the creatures tore into him. She'd watched the light fade from his eyes as his blood seeped into the snow. Then there was just her, and the things that had slaughtered all her friends.

Her leg was broken. There was no question. When she tried to struggle further down the slope, the fierce agony from the movement of her leg made her scream, almost pulling her down into darkness. After a while, she stopped trying to struggle. The cold of the snow seeping through her clothes lessened the pain, numbing her.

At first, Shiv couldn't understand why the creatures didn't just fall on her like they had Malachi and Ryan. After a while, she thought they might be playing with her, like a cat plays with a mouse, savouring the kill. They hovered, metres away, five or six of them, watching her hungrily.

Some time after midnight, she came to realize that it was as if someone had drawn an invisible line in the snow, one the creatures couldn't cross. She knew they wanted her, the longing in their eyes and the way that their jagged nails stretched towards her was proof of that. But something stopped them from getting any nearer to her. They growled and reached, snapped and slavered, but it seemed to Shiv as if an unseen wall blocked their path to her.

All Shiv could do was watch and wait. And somehow that was worse than what had happened to Malachi and Ryan.

At least they hadn't had time to think about

what was about to happen, to analyze it, predict it, imagine the claws and teeth tearing into their flesh. As Shiv sat and shivered and stared, she realized there were two scenarios. In one, she froze to death. In the other, the things somehow found a way to get to her, at her, and they ripped her apart like they had the boys. As she sobbed, her tears solidified on her cheeks like candlewax.

She had been glad of the dark and what she couldn't see, but as dawn approached that changed. The storm lessened, the wind died and light started to creep into the world. The creatures turned from shadows of black and grey into clear, visible figures.

The one that had killed Ryan was the worst. It sat atop its victim's back like an unholy vulture, its bloody claws toying with the ravaged hole in Ryan's coat.

It had once been a man, of that Shiv was fairly sure, but something had happened to it, changed it somehow. Its face was pale and strangely misshapen, framed by a thatch of wild inky hair. Two black, baleful eyes bored into Shiv from under a heavy, angular brow. There was something shark-like about its face, an impression that Shiv realized was made so much worse by its wide, fanged, ghastly mouth. Pieces of Ryan's flesh glistened wet and grisly in the half-light, and her friend's blood ran down the creature's chin on to its tattered green jumper, the kind of thing that an army officer might have worn years before. Ragged bandages covered its hands and its feet, and they flapped and jigged in the wind.

They sat there like that, staring at each other, while other figures danced tantalisingly close to Shiv, reaching for her. Sometimes Shiv slipped asleep, a tiny part of her mind hoping that she would never wake up.

But each time, she did.

Finally, as a tiny ray of light started to illuminate the mountaintop above her, the creatures started to move, backing away into the shadows, dragging Ryan's corpse behind them.

It was only as the first fingers of sunlight danced upon the distant peaks that Shiv felt her eyes close one last time, a blanket of exhaustion slipping over her with a welcome finality.

Chapter Twenty-three

Hanna stared at the ravaged engine, her hope slipping away with her dissipating breath.

It had been a mistake to stay in Kaldgellan.

Hanna had realized it hours before, when the creatures outside the shuttered window had torn apart the boy on the street with a lustful, terrible precision. Whatever they were, whatever Hanna thought she might find out by staying, the time had come to run.

But it seemed that was no longer an option.

They had awoken to a clear sky and no wind. It had tasted like salvation. But within an hour the heavens had turned a sickly, purple hue, a steady trickle of snow starting to fall. It was growing heavier by the minute.

It was just after nine and already the breeze was starting to pick up, a cold, gusting bite that sliced through their clothes.

"Is it fixable?"

Hanna glanced towards Charlie, and gave up trying to mask the anger on her face. She swore, slammed the metal cover back down and stepped away from the snowmobile.

"*Scheisse*! It's a waste of time. They're all the same. The lifts. The pisters. Every bike and tractor we've come across. The engines have been damaged, torn, shredded, the wires ripped out. It would take days to fix them, if they could be fixed at all. *They* know we're still here, somewhere. *They* knew we'd try to run. And *they* made sure we couldn't."

Charlie nodded and stared up disconsolately at the sky. Hanna had spent enough time in the mountains to know that the clouds up there were brimming with snow. There was no way they would be getting down to the valley today.

She felt Charlie's eyes studying her, his voice calm, conciliatory. "So what do we do?"

Hanna reached down and picked up her metal stick from the snow. Before she could stop herself, she let out a shriek of frustration and rage and smashed the end down into the hood of the snowmobile again and again, denting and creasing the metal.

She wasn't sure how long it was before she grew tired of taking her frustrations out on the sled. The sound of her anguish echoed around the empty streets, the noise slowly lessening with each impact. It was a dozen hits before Hanna backed away from the bike, her breath coming in quick gasps. She swore, threw the hockey stick down into the snow and found Charlie staring at her.

"So what do we do? You want to know? What *can* we do? They know we're still here. They're not going to let us go. They're going to kill us. All of us. We got lucky last night. It can't last. On the way over here I saw some new damage to the chalets and houses in the village. Doors wrenched open, windows smashed. You know what I think? Those things are searching for us, once it goes dark. And tonight they're going to find us."

Hanna stared up at the sky, and screamed into the falling snow. "*Scheisse!*"

She turned towards the forests and trees that loomed by the lift station, and started to shout in their direction. "Come on out, you bastards! I know you're there! Come out here in the light, don't make us wait! Do it now! Come on!"

Nothing moved except the flicker of the branches in the wind. The two of them had spent their morning darting from lift station to bike to hut, hiding in shadows and doorways where they could. But any thoughts of subterfuge had fled from Hanna when she began her frantic assault on the snowmobile.

Charlie bent down and picked up Hanna's hockey stick. He stared at Hanna for a moment then reached out for her hand. When she hesitated, Charlie nodded in the direction of an old, grizzled bar across the street and reached out for her again.

She didn't know what he had in mind, but she took his fingers all the same, blinded by a sudden wave of fatigue and hopelessness.

The entrance to the bar was latched, a few feet of snow piled against the wood down by their feet, but when Charlie tried the door it groaned open. He pushed at the gnarled wood gently then stepped inside, glancing around the darkened room. A stink of smoke, stale beer and damp drifted to Hanna's nostrils. But apart from glistening patches of broken glass on the floor and a few overturned chairs, the place was empty and still.

Charlie gestured at a worn sofa by the entrance.

Hanna had barely slept the night before, and the scuffed leather felt soft and welcoming as she parked herself down.

She watched as Charlie walked over to the bar, took down two small glasses, then turned and scrutinized the bottles that lined the far wall. He hesitated for a moment, took one of the spirits down, and poured what was probably far too much into both glasses. Then he made his way back round the bar towards Hanna. She raised her eyebrows questioningly.

"Trying to get me drunk?"

Charlie shook his head and put a glass in front of her. "When we lived by the sea my dad used to come home sometimes from one of his shifts, when he was out on the lifeboats, and if he'd had a bad one he'd pour himself a big glass of whatever we had in the house. Sometimes he told me they'd been too late and they'd had to fish bodies out of the sea. I think it got to him, though he never showed it. But he said a drink was good. Said it got rid of the shakes. I always remember him saying that. I wouldn't really know whisky from gin, but Stefan brought us in here on the first day, had one of these after a day's skiing. And it seemed to do the job for him."

Hanna glanced at Charlie warily, then reached out and picked up the glass.

"To Stefan, then. *Prost!*"

She took a long, deep gulp, then coughed and shook her head. The alcohol tasted sharp and bitter, but even though it burned Hanna all the way down, she felt a little of her fatigue and anger fade away in a burst of warmth.

Hanna felt a smile tug at her lips. "Stefan always did have the poorest taste in alcohol."

She stared at Charlie and nodded down at his drink. He hacked and coughed as he swallowed, but he downed it all the same, then glanced cautiously up at Hanna. "So were you and Stefan…?"

Hanna shook her head at the question. "No. Never. He wanted to, but he wasn't my type. Too *selbstgefallig*, too … smug? Liked himself too much. A nice guy, but not for me."

She fell silent, her eyes wandering around at the faded walls of the pub.

"He was like me, though, an outsider. I grew up here but moved away when I was little. And Stefan used to come here as a child for holidays, but he came back here to work whenever he had breaks from university. I can't believe he's gone. I can't believe any of this."

She fell silent for a moment, then picked up her glass and held it up to the light. "You were right. My shakes have gone already. To your father. *Prost*."

She took a fresh hit from her drink, felt her face twist into a grimace, and finished off the little that was left before giving Charlie a curious look. "But I'm not the only one who's an outsider. It doesn't take a genius to work out that the rest of those from your school don't trust you. And the angry one, Jordan, he keeps referring to you as a criminal. You going to tell me why?"

Charlie's face reddened and Hanna found herself noticing, not for the first time, how there was something about him, something edgily attractive. Hanna became aware that she was staring and she quickly averted her eyes, leaning back in her chair and moving her attention to a photograph of the mountain that sat above Charlie's head on the faded wall. A handful of tiny figures stood on a deserted piste in the black and white picture. Charlie's words dragged her back to the tatty lounge.

"You said if we made it through the night you'd tell me what happened to your brother."

Hanna felt the warm glow of alcohol slip away. "And I thought you just wanted to sit here and get drunk with me."

She took a deep breath. "If you want to hear about Jon, you're going to have to pour us another drink. We both know we're not getting out of Kaldgellan, not today anyway. I'm going to go back to the hotel after this and I'm going to close my eyes for a while. I'm out of ideas. I'm exhausted. And another drink might just help me sleep."

Charlie nodded and made his way to the bar. He looked unsteady on his feet, but he managed to pour them both another glass.

Hanna studied him as he sat down. She had no desire to tell her story, but neither did she want to go out into the storm, or back to the ominous silence of the decaying hostel. And she found herself wanting to know more about the haunted young man that somehow reminded her so much of herself.

"OK, so I'll make you a deal. I'll tell you about my brother if you tell me why they call you a criminal.

And what happened to your father. I'm no genius, but the look on your face when you talk about him reminds me of how I feel when I think about Jon. We have a deal?"

Charlie held her eyes for a moment and shrugged. "OK, whatever. It's not the most exciting of stories, but I'll tell you if you really want to know."

Hanna glanced over her shoulder, towards the door. The snow was much heavier again outside, the wind thudding against the door. She rose from the sofa, latched the door gently then sat back down. Thin beams of light shone in through the bars on the windows, illuminating the dancing motes of dust.

"We can't stay here too long. But right now there's nowhere else we need to be."

Charlie nodded and Hanna took a quick swig of her drink, fought back a cough and slipped back into the past.

"Jon loved this shitty little village. We grew up here then moved away nearer to Innsbruck when I was five or six. You know Kaldgellan by now. You've seen it all, I think. There's not a lot to see. There's nothing here but snow in the winter, grass in the summer. I was glad to get away from here, to somewhere with a little bit of life in it. But Jon missed this place. He said he felt like life was simpler here. When he was seventeen, he found some work in one of the valleys nearby. Taking experienced skiers on the slopes in the winter, doing tours and hiking in the summer. He loved it. He was much older than me, and a real ... free spirit. The last time I saw him was at Christmas, a decade ago now. I'd just started attending a boarding school near the city, and I couldn't wait to get home for the holidays and see him. We went ice skating in Innsbruck, visited the Christmas markets. Touristy stuff but so special."

She paused and licked her lips, then took another sip of her drink. Outside, a gust of wind sent snow billowing down the street like a sandstorm. Hanna looked out of the barred window and shivered.

"I was back at school when my parents came to tell me the news. Jon had been in the west of the valley, at another peak a mile or two from here, taking a school party off-piste. He was an excellent guide, careful, steady, an outstanding skier. It still doesn't make sense to me. An avalanche, they said. Killed all twelve students he was with, Jon as well.

Swept them right down the mountain. Tore them apart. He was eighteen, a year older than I am now. By the time my parents and I made it out here, it was all over. We had a small service then I went back to school. My parents, they never really got over it."

Charlie nodded. "I'm sorry."

Hanna shrugged and played with the ring in her nose. "It was a long time ago now. But like my parents, I don't think I ever moved past it."

"So why did you come back here?"

Hanna felt her guard come up, a line drawn in the sand that she wasn't willing to cross. Matthias's words from the day before the storm echoed in her mind, the fear shining in his eyes.

She couldn't quite bring herself to meet Charlie's eyes when she replied. "I'm still not sure. I came back when I was fifteen, worked across the valley, in kitchens, bars. Part of me wanted to see this place again. To try and get it straight up here." She tapped the shaven side of her head with a savagely bitten fingernail.

"Then when I came to Kaldgellan I just felt closer to him. To Jon. I found myself talking to him when I

182

was up in the mountains. A little later I got a job as a guide, mostly showing rich hikers around the passes and runs, making sure they didn't kill themselves. I was only going to do it for a year. But I never left."

She caught Charlie's eyes and breathed out slowly. He didn't believe her, she was sure of it, just in the same way she felt certain that he was the type of person that kept more than a few secrets of his own.

"Now I'm not sure I ever will. So. That's my story. That's why I'm here. Your turn."

Charlie nodded resignedly, swallowed a mouthful of his drink and coughed. "What do you want to know?"

Hanna watched him like a hawk. "All of it."

Charlie picked up both of their glasses, stumbled towards the bar, filled them again, and made his way back and slumped into his seat.

"I moved around a lot as a kid. My mum died when I was little, I never really knew her, and my dad found it hard to settle, I guess. I learned to snowboard when we moved to the Scottish highlands. My dad worked as a tree surgeon, and in the winters he'd take me out on to the snow. He tried to teach me to ski, but I couldn't get it at all.

Then one day he strapped me on a board and it just came naturally. After that, it was just the two of us, exploring, being in the mountains. I remember it as being pretty perfect. Then we moved to a little village up at the very tip of Scotland. My dad loved to surf and the waves there were really special. We started to make friends, settle a little, and through somebody he met out in the waves he got offered a job as a lifeguard, working the boats, the water patrol."

He paused, his eyes far away, and Hanna could tell that Charlie didn't want to go on, that it was an effort just to get the words out.

"One night there was a bad storm, so strong that the tide took out the houses at the front of our village, came straight over the seawall. The electricity went out all along the coast, the lines went down. It was bad. A trawler got into trouble out at sea just before dawn, and my dad got the call to go. He hugged me before he went out, just as I went off to school. I remember the briny smell that clung to him, the feel of his grizzled beard. I never saw him again."

Charlie shrugged neutrally, but Hanna could

recognize only too well how the memories still gnawed away at him.

"At his funeral a week later one of the other crew members told me that he died trying to rescue a guy who'd been swept overboard. Being selfless, like he always said. Dad went into the water to try to fish someone out. Neither of them made it. Ben, the guy from the lifeguard crew, told me my dad didn't think twice, just went. I have a grandmother, down in Bristol. After the funeral, I moved the little stuff I had down in with her."

Hanna's found herself studying him anew, the mystery of their first encounter starting to fall into place. "So that day we met ... is that why you didn't care? When you were out there on the mountain ... because of your dad?"

Charlie shrugged and shifted uneasily.

"What about your gran? I mean, wouldn't she miss you? Aren't you all she has left?"

Charlie shook his head, his face betraying the conflict within. His eyes looked torn, pained, and tears glistened in the dark when he finally spoke.

"I've never told anyone this. But so far keeping it in has just got me into more and more trouble.

So screw it. My gran's sick. Alzheimer's. She doesn't have long. So I don't have a lot to go home for. Last time I saw her, just before I left, she didn't even really know who I was. They were in the process of putting her into a home, and me... Who knows. I wasn't sure whether to come out here or not, but my tutor, he got it and he knew that things weren't so good for me at home. He put in a word for me, pulled some strings, so that they let me on the trip, despite all the shit I've done. I used my dad's money to pay for it, the little bit he left for me. And when I got here, I realized I'd not really been living for a while. That's where I was when we met, I guess. I didn't care any more. And I really didn't want to go home."

Charlie's eyes met hers and Hanna found herself battling against a wave of feelings.

Ones she couldn't afford to accommodate.

She forced the emotion away from her face. "Well, now you might not have to. So what were they, these things you did, that Jordan and the others talk to you the way they do?"

Charlie closed his eyes, shook his head and heaved himself up from his chair. "Some other time."

Chapter Twenty-four

Tara was staring at her phone screen when Poppy's croaked mumblings made her look up. On the sofa across from her, Poppy sounded like she'd been crawling across some arid desert, starved of water. Cold beads of sweat shone on her forehead.

For a moment Poppy lingered at the edge of sleep, then she opened her eyes and glanced up blearily at Tara. It seemed to take her a while to come back into the room and Tara wondered if the strange hallucinations she'd complained of earlier that morning were still plaguing her. She sighed, switched off her phone and gazed in Poppy's direction.

"So the voices ... are they still there?"

A little at a time, the confusion slipped from Poppy's face and she nodded slowly. "They come and go. But some of the things they say aren't nice."

Poppy tried on a stoic smile, but it didn't reach

her eyes. Tara felt a prickle of unease, and she found herself trying to keep a little distance from the other girl and the possibility of some weird infection from the bite.

"But it's just a fever, right? That's what Hanna reckoned. Once they find us, once someone comes, they'll fix you up, bandage your leg and you'll be fine, won't you?"

Poppy's lack of answer spoke volumes. She swallowed dryly and nodded at Tara's phone. "Anything?"

"Nothing. I've not been able to get any signal since the day it started snowing. Since the day everyone vanished. I can't even make an emergency call. And now I'm pretty sure my battery's going to die next time I switch it on."

She leaned her head back against the sofa and glanced over at Poppy's ankle, where blood still seeped slowly through the material. "How's your leg?"

Poppy reached her pale fingers down towards the wound. "It hurts. And I'm so, so tired. I can't do any more than hobble, so unless those two find something that can carry me off the mountain, I won't be going anywhere. But the pain's bearable as long as I keep doped up on painkillers."

Tara nodded absently, her attention caught by a movement out beyond the shutters. They had made a rough camp of sorts on the first floor of the decaying hostel and a growing pile of debris was starting to develop on the floorboards. Hanna had scavenged some more cans of food at first light, and the empties lay derelict on the floor, among a few bottles of water and a pile of sleeping bags and duvets.

Nico had insisted that they let a little light into the lounge, just for their own sanity, and Tara stood and placed her hands on the shutters, opening them a fraction more. She blinked against the daylight, watching the whirling flakes outside, then she shook her head and came and sat back down next to Poppy.

"Nothing. Maybe those two ran away together. Maybe they realized that we're not going to survive another night and they made a break for it." She realized what she was saying. "Do you … do you think they did?"

Poppy shook her head slowly. "No. I don't know

189

Hanna very well, but no matter what Charlie did or didn't do back at home, I don't think he'd do that. Where are the others?"

As if in reply to her words, Ellie padded in through the doorway, glanced around, then looked across at Tara. "Nico's gone for a sleep. He's lucky, I've been trying, but there was no way. Jordan and Leandra went to get some more water. Nobody really wanted to go outside but we're nearly out. I thought the storm had gone this morning, that help would come, but it's started again, hasn't it? It's worse than ever now. How long can it last?"

Tara turned away and watched as Poppy wiped a fresh fusillade of sweat away from her brow.

"I don't know. But those things didn't find us last night, even though they were right outside. Somebody is going to come soon, surely. Ryan will have made it. And it's been nearly three days since we spoke to anybody on the outside. Surely they'll come soon."

Ellie wrapped her arms around herself. "Not soon enough."

Poppy glanced across at Tara. "You know, they might be on their way up here right now. Ryan and the others, they might have made it down to the valley, raised the alarm, got help. They could be here any minute."

Tara chewed at her bottom lip and felt a fresh burst of hope slip over her like a blanket. "I saw a film a few months ago. It was about a mountain, Everest, a place a lot of dumb people wanted to climb. I watched it with Ryan, over at his mum's place. We didn't go out in public too much. We weren't really supposed to be together. He's from the wrong part of the city, you know, those flats, over in St Paul's? My parents would never have let me anywhere near him so we had to keep it secret. But Ryan was always really nice to me. He made me feel better about things, my mum and dad, losing all our money. And he liked me for me."

She stared away wistfully for a moment, then slipped back to what she had been saying. "The film he chose for us to watch, it had this scene where a storm came in and all the people climbing the mountain got caught in it. A lot of them froze, just died out in the cold. And that film, the storm, looked just like this. But some of them, they made it. It took them days. But they made it to safety. And

Ryan, he's going to make it."

She glanced up at the window. The sky was slowly darkening, black clouds obscuring the mountains in the distance. "I hate that skinny black-haired girl, Hanna. And I'm sick of being told what to do by her, bossed around."

Tara chewed at a rogue nail, then glanced across at Ellie. "You're brave, you know. You haven't seemed scared through all of this."

Ellie played with one of the rings on her finger, twisting it round self-consciously. "Trust me, I have been. But where I grew up, it wasn't always pretty. I've seen some heavy things. Nothing like this, but there's rarely a day that goes by without a fight, a mugging, someone getting stabbed or beaten up."

Tara kept her eyes fixed on the other girl. "We never really talked, did we? But I saw your fashion work, the stuff you did in textiles, at that show after school in November. It was stunning."

Tara paused for a moment, and a slow blush swept across Ellie's cheeks.

"You think so? It's what I want to do, you know. Fashion. I mean, what I wanted to do. Before ... this."

Tara nodded slowly. "You're really talented, you

know. And too clever to let that Austrian skank tell you what to do. Next time she starts throwing her weight around, maybe we should make a stand, tell her what we really think."

Tara reckoned Ellie looked flattered by the compliment from someone so many leagues above her socially, but there was still a fraction of uncertainty on her face. Tara sensed that her campaign was gaining momentum and pressed on.

"And maybe, if those things come out again tonight, tomorrow we should just tell Hanna where to stick it, and walk or ski as far away as we can get. Anything is better than being stuck here."

Poppy sighed loudly, disrupting Tara's takeover bid. "I don't have a choice."

Tara looked back at Poppy, then peered dubiously at the bandage, noticing the odd, sweet smell that seemed to linger around it. "So these voices ... are they talking now?"

Poppy nodded slowly, her eyes far away. "They're in my head. Like a radio, drifting in from miles away, fuzzy and garbled. Half of their words I can't understand. And the ones I can... What they're saying isn't nice. And the things they're telling me to do, I—"

Tara didn't hear the rest of what Poppy was saying because she heard voices too, drifting up from the street below.

She quickly stood up and moved to the window, her heart thumping in her chest like a hammer. "There's something moving out there. Two figures. I think it's them. I think they're back."

Chapter Twenty-five

A weight on the edge of the bed woke Charlie up.

He had fallen asleep picturing Hanna, the haunted shine in the grey of her eyes, the way her face had lit up in the bar when he had finally seen her smile. The more time Charlie spent with her, the more he felt that there was something between them, something a little more than a desperate co-dependence.

After they had left the bar, Hanna and Charlie had weaved their way back through the storm to the hostel. Charlie hadn't been able to stop yawning as they told the others about the damage to the lifts and the snowmobiles. It had been three days, he'd realized, since he'd had any real sleep, and he was starting to feel ill with exhaustion, shivery and sick. He had found an old dormitory on the first floor and fallen on to the bed nearest the door. Covering himself with a sleeping bag, he had been asleep in seconds.

He awoke to find the room darker, the walls greyer. Charlie guessed it was some time after lunch. He wiped at his eyes and looked towards the end of the bed.

Leandra was sitting there. Her long black hair hung loose and a blanket covered her from her shoulders down to her feet. A shy smile flickered on her lips, but tears brimmed in her eyes.

"Sorry for waking you. I wanted to sleep but I couldn't. I was just sick of sitting down there, looking out at the storm, waiting for it to go dark again. Sick of being scared."

Charlie sat up, yawned, rubbed at an itch on his scalp. "That's OK. I was only dozing. You don't have to be sorry."

Leandra shook her head. She seemed to be shaking a little, though Charlie wasn't sure it was from the cold. She shuffled a millimetre closer to Charlie, and it was as if her nervous energy thrummed along the bed in his direction.

"I wanted to say sorry for lying to you the other night. It wasn't Fatima that liked you. It was me. I didn't want ... didn't want to get to tonight without telling you. And I wanted to feel something other than scared."

Charlie felt his mouth go dry. Leandra's hand fell on his and his heartbeat started to hammer in his chest.

"I've always liked you. From the first day you came into my class. I've thought about you a lot, wondered what it would be like to..." Leandra trailed off and a sad smile flickered on her lips. "I wasn't ever going to tell you. But it doesn't matter any more, does it?"

Charlie started to speak just as Leandra leaned forwards and placed her mouth on his. Her lips felt soft and warm, and she moved her hand and placed it at the back of his neck, holding him locked against her. Charlie's heart felt like it might rip its way out of his ribcage and he pulled away from her.

Leandra's eyes swam with confusion. Her mouth formed a single word. "Please."

She brushed her lips against his again before he could reply. Her movements were hungrier now, more urgent. Charlie found himself kissing her back, felt her tongue run over his teeth. Her hands were in his hair, their bodies jammed together and he could feel her breath coming in fast, heavy gasps. He put his fingers up to her face, feeling her tears on his fingertips.

She pulled away from him, her chest rising and falling quickly. Her dark eyes bored into his. "I want you. Can we…"

She didn't finish, but instead she kissed him again, her hands on his chest, then his stomach, then lower, until he felt her starting to undo the zip on his jeans. Charlie felt like he was being swept along on a wave, one he couldn't stop.

A forceful knocking made them pull abruptly away from each other. Charlie looked up and saw Hanna's face peering at him through the gap in the door. He felt strangely guilty and his face flushed red.

Hanna lingered by the door, staring at the two of them. It was a few seconds before she spoke. "Am I disturbing something?"

Leandra glanced at Charlie, rose up from the bed, and pushed past Hanna and out into the corridor.

Hanna took a step into the room. "I'm sorry if I did. But there's something I need you to see. It's important. Get your coat on and come with me."

Chapter Twenty-six

"Where are we going?"

Charlie could barely make out his own words above the storm. He'd trailed Hanna to a handyman's store where they'd picked up some supplies she thought they might need, including a crowbar that she'd handed ominously to Charlie. Now she was marching him towards a small group of chalets that sat at the edge of Kaldgellan, just before the mountain fell into the valley far below.

He doubted that Hanna would hear him at all, but she turned back and lowered the scarf that covered her mouth. The battered hockey stick was in her other hand. The sight of its bloody tip made Charlie want to turn and run back to the hostel.

"While you were getting cosy with your girlfriend, I was up on the second floor and I saw something. A light, in one of the chalets. It was on for a while then it went off. I thought I could use your help. Now

I'm not so sure I should have bothered. You and that girl, Leandra. Have you two done that before?"

Charlie felt his face redden anew and he shook his head. "No. I'd never spoken to her before this trip, not really. I didn't see that coming. I just … I woke up and she was there."

Hanna stared at him, a glimmer of mistrust in her eyes. Her voice was neutral but she seemed agitated. "How lovely for you both. Well, I'm sorry I got in the way. We won't be long. It looked like it was about to get serious. You two can always pick up where you left off once we're back."

Charlie shook his head. "I don't think so."

Hanna started off again into the wall of snow. "Come on. It's going to be dusk in an hour or two. And there's no way we want to be outside after dark. Follow me."

The snowfall seemed heavier than ever and Charlie was constantly wiping at his face with wet gloves. The drifts they slogged through were waist-deep in places and he found himself sweating at the exertion. They turned a corner around the side of a whitewashed cottage and Hanna grabbed Charlie by the shoulder, pulling him down alongside her so that they crouched among the drifts.

"There! See it, just there, that chalet on the left. There's a light in there, candles or a lantern. Look!"

Charlie blinked through the falling snow, trying to pick out what Hanna was pointing at. In front of them were some of the more modern buildings in Kaldgellan, a row of chalets that faced the village but backed on to the sheer drop that fell away to the floor of the valley miles beneath.

At first Charlie couldn't see what Hanna meant, then he spotted it, an orange glow that shimmered in the centre of the long bay window. "You think there's somebody in there?"

Hanna nodded. "That day everyone vanished, I couldn't understand where the villagers had gone. I thought they'd been taken by those things. But what if that's one of them? It might be a signal, another survivor. Or it might be one of your friends, somebody else who got away. Come on."

As they reached the door, Hanna gestured for Charlie to stay put, then she crawled across and peered up through the bottom of the window. She watched for a moment, then ducked down and made her way back to Charlie.

"I can't see anybody. There's a living room there, some lit candles in the corner, but no sign of life."

"So what do we do?"

"We need to take a look inside."

The echo of Charlie's feet on the floorboards seemed far too loud as he followed Hanna out of the storm. The inside of the chalet was a nest of shadows and gloom. Fresh logs sat piled up in a clean hearth and on the mantelpiece above them faded black-and-white photographs seemed to move in the light from the dancing candles.

Charlie pushed the door to, cutting off the wind, and crept closer to the hearth. The frames showed family photographs taken in the village and the surrounding valleys. They were drained of colour, their definition slowly decaying from years on display. As Hanna stepped into the next room, Charlie picked up one of the pictures, brushed off the dust and brought it closer to the light so that he could see the faces of the people in the photograph.

"*Guten Nachmittag.*"

Charlie jumped at the words and swore out loud. The photograph leaped from his fingers. It hit the stone floor and sent tiny fragments of glass spinning away in a dozen different directions.

The unknown voice came from behind him, in the next room along.

Charlie turned and darted after Hanna, pausing at the entrance to a small kitchen.

An old man sat in an armchair in the corner of the room. He was wearing a battered sheepskin jacket, and his grey hair hung down on to a fur-lined collar. There was a table in front of him, with a bottle of whisky standing upon it, half empty. The stranger smiled at Charlie, but the warmth of the expression didn't drift up to the old man's eyes.

Behind him, a sink and a few kitchen counters gave way to a huge bay window with what would have been a stunning view of the valley below. Today, though, the tiny streets and villages far beneath them were obscured by the snow and cloud.

"*Schön, nicht wahr?*"

Charlie's eyes flicked across to Hanna. "What did he say?"

The old man glanced at Charlie. His face looked impossibly old and lined, his blue eyes dull and faded. There was a flicker of recognition in them as he examined Charlie.

"English, aren't you? I haven't spoken English for years. I've made it a point not to mix with the few visitors we have had to Kaldgellan in recent times."

The old man reached down and picked up a glass of whisky that sat next to the bottle. He took a sip and smiled again, the lines on his face growing deeper with the expression.

"You must be one of the school party I saw arriving last week, a few days before the storm came in. And you," his eyes slowly slid towards Hanna, "you're the guide, aren't you? I've seen you before, over the past few months. I remember your brother."

Hanna took a step closer to him, the hockey stick still held tightly in her fingers. "Who are you? Why are you here?"

"My name is Wolfgang. I've always lived here, in this mountain range, but I settled in Kaldgellan more than thirty years ago. I've seen the winters come and go. I've seen many like you. But you two have done well. What is it now, two days? Three? You've done well to stay alive so long."

Charlie had been looking around the room, but suddenly his attention switched squarely to the old man. His heart seemed to thump in his throat and he stepped into the dining room and stared at the stranger.

"You know what's going on? You know what those things are?"

The old man smiled. "I hoped you would come. Usually, their hunt only lasts a day, two at the most. But you and your friends have evaded them. I lit the candles to try to draw you here, to talk to you. How many of you are there left?"

Charlie felt scared now, more scared than he'd been the night before when he had listened to the screams of the boy out on the street. Somehow the old man, his words, were more real than anything that had come before. Charlie's voice shook when he spoke again. "You didn't answer the question. What are those things?"

"This place is cursed. This whole mountaintop, the neighbouring peaks. You may not know, but this is the most remote region of the Austrian Alps. There's a reason *they* were trapped here."

The old man took a deep breath, collected himself for a moment then looked up at the visitors.

"My first memory of them is from when I was a little boy. I still remember my parents hurrying to get my little sister and myself away from the mountains, down to the valley below. I remember the fear in my father's eyes. It's funny what stays with you. So many things I've forgotten, but not that day. I knew something was wrong. I might not have understood, but I knew."

Hanna took a step closer, the stick raised threateningly. "What is going on? Where's everyone gone? Tell us!"

The old man waved at a hand at the valley below. "Down there, the people know nothing. I envy them. They carry on with their little lives, oblivious. They suspect, perhaps, that this place is haunted, blighted. That's why so few outsiders come here now. Because every few years *they* come out again. Even though the people down in the valley don't know what it is, they can sense the evil on the wind."

Hanna tapped the table with the tip of her hockey stick, splashing droplets of whisky from the tumbler. When she spoke, there was a trace of fear in her words. "You *tell* us, old man, you tell us what is going on."

"The first time they came in my lifetime, as I said, I was a boy. There were many times before, my grandfather told me, but that was the first I knew of them. I don't know how many lives it took to satisfy them but they slept for many years after that. They next came when I was a man, thirty years later. Then again a score of years after that. The last time they came must have been no more than ten years ago. Now they come again. And this time you are the sacrifices."

Outside, the light had started to fade, the trees along the mountainside bathed in blue shadows. Apart from the howl of the wind as it whipped around the side of the chalet, there was a deathly silence.

Charlie's mouth felt so dry he could barely get the words out. "What are they?"

The old man carried on as if he hadn't heard the question. "The last time they grew hungry, they fed on the next mountaintop, a few miles from here. An avalanche, we told the world. A dozen outsiders taken by the mountain. But it wasn't an avalanche. It was *them*. Twenty years before that the story was told that it was a plane that came down. But there was no plane wreckage. No plane at all. It was *them*. We have kept their secret. Just so long as they let us live."

Hanna swore, the words loud and angry in the dim light. "What are they? What do we do?"

The old man shook his head gravely. "What do you do? You die. They won't lift this storm until they have you all, not now they have your scent. Tonight. Tomorrow. They will hunt you down. You've done well to last this long."

Charlie felt the floorboards squeak under his feet as he took a wary step closer. "What are they?"

"We do not speak of them lest our words wake them, not unless it's to warn each other that their time is here again. We hear their voices in our dreams. Their stirring whispers let us know that they are wakening. *The Lost Ones*, my father called them. Monsters."

Hanna swore again, and spat her words at the old man. "There's no such thing!"

The old man raised his grey eyebrows and smiled. "We both know there are. They are ancient. My grandparents told me they were cursed to spend eternity in a living death, that they can never return to what they were. Just as they can never set foot off these mountains. But whatever they may be, they are hungry again. And you are their prey."

He pointed at a gnarled oak door at the back of the kitchen. "They don't want me, but all the same, I have not dared show my face at night. I'd rather freeze and shiver down in the darkness than face them. The sound of them is more than enough for me."

Charlie looked out at the looming dark. "What can we do? How do we survive?"

"You don't. The sooner they find you, the sooner this storm will lift. The townsfolk will creep back to their houses, a story will be told to the world, another avalanche, perhaps, or a coach crash, or a faulty lift that sent a cable car crashing to the ground. Nobody will be any the wiser. And *they* will sleep again."

He glanced up at the grandfather clock that hung above the cooker. "But you should go now, go back to wherever you've been hiding. They will come for you tonight. Enjoy the dusk. It will be the last one you see."

Hanna cursed and swept her stick across the table. It sent the bottle smashing against the nearest wall where it shattered in an explosion of glass and whisky.

The old man watched the ochre droplets slide steadily down the wall, his face serene and still. "There's more in my cellar. Enough to last me tonight."

Hanna took a step closer. "I should kill you, you evil bastard! You say you've known about this for years! This is your fault! You could have stopped this. I should do the world a favour!"

The old man's fingers disappeared into his pocket and he pulled out a bottle of tablets. "You don't need to. I don't plan to sit here and listen to their howls again tonight. I'll do it myself. There's only so many sins one soul can bear."

He undid the cap, shook out a handful of small capsules and reached for the little whisky that was left in his glass. Then he placed the capsules into his mouth, swallowed and looked back up at his visitors. "I would do the same if I was you."

Hanna swore at him and grabbed hold of Charlie's arm. "You're wrong. We won't die. Come on, Charlie, leave the old man to rot. Leave him to go to hell."

She started to march towards the door, but froze

and slowly turned round. "You said last time it was an avalanche. Not far from here. When?"

The old man's voice drifted to Charlie's ears. "Ten years ago. The year your brother died. He didn't deserve his fate. None of them did."

Hanna swore, lifted the hockey stick and stormed towards the old man. Before she could swing for him Charlie caught her wrist.

"No. He isn't worth it. You're better than he is."

Her grey eyes were blazing and for a moment he thought she might swing for him instead. Charlie put his arms around her. "Leave him. Come on. He isn't worth it. He isn't."

Hanna took a deep breath and glanced at the old man one last time. "You're wrong, old man. You're going to hell. But we're going to live."

Then she stalked back outside into the storm.

Chapter Twenty-seven

Hanna didn't bother to check that Charlie was with her as she made her way back to the hostel. Her head raged with the old man's words and she found herself wishing she had caused him more than a little pain before the tablets did their work.

They passed the awning of a butcher's shop, the hooks hanging empty behind the glass. Before she knew what she was doing, Hanna turned to the right, pushed open the door and stepped inside, the bell above the doorway ringing merrily.

The interior of the shop stank, a high odour of dried blood and salted meat. She heard Charlie follow her into the store, his fingers clicking on the switch by the door. Hanna heard the back-up generator kick in and a bar of lights on the ceiling blinked and flickered into life, bathing the room in a bleached electric glow.

Hanna stalked over to the till, ran her hands

through her hair and found her reflection staring back from the cold metal of the counter. Somewhere a heavy door clanged in the wind. Charlie took a step towards the back of the shop, but Hanna shook her head wearily.

"Don't worry. I checked this place two days ago when I was with Stefan. There's a meat storage locker at the back and nothing else."

She heard herself swear, closed her eyes. "I just need a minute."

Charlie moved alongside her and placed a hand on her shoulder. She heard his voice, calm, steady. "No matter what he said, you did the right thing. You kill him, you're as bad as he is."

Hanna opened her eyes. Her chest burned with a mixture of despair and anger, and she felt her fingers curl into fists.

"It's not that. I knew something was coming. And I could have run. I *should* have run. But something kept me here."

Charlie's dark eyes bored into her. "What do you mean? What did you know?"

Hanna realized the time for secrets had passed long ago. "The instructor. The older one, Matthias.

He's always looked out for me. And he spoke to me, the day before the storm came in. He said I needed to leave. Said he couldn't tell me why, but just that I should go. He was scared. Shaking. But I knew I couldn't leave. I had the strangest feeling that if I stayed, I might find out what happened to my brother. That's why I came back. I needed to know. I knew Jon couldn't have died in an avalanche. But now I'm going to die, aren't I? Just like Jon did. We might as well take a stack of tablets from the chemist over there and do what that old bastard did! We're dead, aren't we? We'd be just as good if we'd gone with Ryan and the others out into the storm. At least that would be cleaner than letting those things … *Scheisse*!"

Hanna bit back a cry of pain as her knuckles slammed on the counter. Charlie took a step closer to her so that only inches separated them.

"You asked me, at the bar earlier, what I'd done and why Jordan called me a criminal. Why the others kept away from me. You still want to know?"

Hanna nodded numbly.

"Back when my gran got diagnosed, when I knew it wouldn't be long, when I knew I was going to lose the only person I had left, I got angry. So angry I did some stupid things. It started with shoplifting. Magazines. Clothes. Stuff from school. I didn't even want the things I took. I just wanted someone to notice me. But nobody did. So one night I stole a car, clipped a van, smashed into a tree. Maybe I just wanted to get away from my shitty life in the city. Or maybe I wanted to get caught. I just wanted someone to realize that I wasn't OK, that I wasn't coping. But people got hurt. And all I did was make things worse, get a criminal record. But you want to know what the worst thing is?"

Hanna shook her head, picturing Charlie back in the city, trying to keep his head above water.

"My dad. He'd have been disgusted with me. I let him down. He was all about protecting people, not putting them in danger. Maybe that's why I stayed, when Ryan left, when the others went. My dad would have stayed. That was what he did. Whatever it cost him. Maybe I thought that by staying, I could make things up to him, make him proud again."

Hanna heard a choked cry slip from her lips. "You'll find out soon enough. You're going to die up here."

Charlie took a deep breath and nodded slowly. "Maybe. Maybe we both are. But maybe we can choose how we go. We can lie down, wait for those things to find us. Or we can try and stay alive. I know what my dad would want me to do. What would your brother want you to do?"

Charlie's words burned away at Hanna, and she realized there was truth in what he said.

She turned to Charlie and found it was no longer despair that made her voice shake. Suddenly she saw that there was another way, a way to quell the anger that had dragged her back to Kaldgellan. "You know what I want? I want to find those things, smash them, kill them, kill every last one of them. If that old bastard was right, they murdered my brother. And I've mourned him every day for ten years, turned my back on everything, everybody, and now…"

Charlie took her hand in his and Hanna realized again how similar they were, and how separate pasts of pain and suffering now somehow bound them together.

"Do it, then. Do whatever it takes for us to get through this. Look outside. The storm's lessening, the snowfall's nearly stopped. Maybe we can make it."

Hanna nodded, picked up her hockey stick and wiped the snow off its edge.

"If those things come after us tonight, if they find us, I'll make them sorry. I'll take as many with me as I can. Come on. We need to make one more stop before we get back to the hostel."

Chapter Twenty-eight

Nico found himself reeling at Hanna's words. "Are you insane? If those things get in here, we need to run. We have to!"

"If you run, you're dead. We've seen them out there. We can't outrun them, not in the open. They're like wolves. They would be on you in seconds. But you're welcome to try."

Across from Nico, Ellie's eyes widened in horror. "We can't fight them. That's the last thing we should do. We need to hide and keep hidden. If what that old man told you is true, they're hunting us. Didn't you see what they did to our friends back at the hotel?"

Hanna glanced at Ellie coldly. "I saw. I saw it all, from the moment they took Stefan. And I remember leading you all to safety that night. If I hadn't led you upstairs you'd have been eaten along with your friends. At least my way we have a chance."

Tara swore, stepped away from the shutters and sat down with the others. A strand of her long blond hair slipped down over her face, and she pushed it back from her eyes. "I agree with Ellie. A chance of what? Of making them angry? How do we even know we can hurt those things?"

Charlie and Hanna had returned from the village streets with a bag of stale loaves and baguettes salvaged from a bakery. Tough as it was, the bread still tasted heavenly after three days of tinned food. As they recounted their conversation with the old man, Nico couldn't help but wonder if they had brought it to soften the blow of the story they had to tell.

Nico's appetite had faded as Charlie recounted the old man's words. And a moment later his poor stomach threatened to regurgitate the little bread he had eaten when Hanna unveiled her plans in the event of the creatures finding their way into the hostel.

It was fair to say her strategy hadn't gone down well. But, as ever, Hanna didn't seem to care too much what the others thought.

"I know we can hurt them."

Tara snorted. "What, have you got a crystal ball as well?"

Hanna shook her head dismissively. "I know."

"Really? How?"

Hanna narrowed her eyes and glanced across at Tara. "I killed one."

Leandra leaned forwards and joined the conversation. "What? When?"

"The day when Ryan left. When I went into the ski shop to check it was clear, there was one of those things pinned under the wheels of the bus. The one that bit *her*."

Nico watched as Poppy seemed to come out of a daze. She didn't seem well at all, her face pale, her eyes feverish, and she had hardly left the sofa in the past twenty-four hours. Her brow was constantly beaded with sweat and there were dark lines under her eyes.

She sat up a little and squinted across at Hanna. "You saw it ... the one that bit me?"

"It was like a shark that had washed up on a beach. Black eyes full of hate and hunger. A wide mouth, dozens of jagged, bloody teeth. Your blood."

Poppy wiped at her eyes as if rubbing away

sleep. "What did you do to it?"

Hanna shrugged and nodded down at the metal hockey stick that went everywhere with her. "I made sure it wouldn't bite anyone else. I smashed away at that thing until all that was left were bones and brains and skull and teeth. Trust me, they can be killed."

Tara wrapped her coat around her shoulders. "What are you, some kind of robot? Everyone else is terrified, and you're going on about killing them. What's wrong with you?"

Hanna waved Tara's words away dismissively. "If they come here tonight, I'll try to kill some more."

As if to emphasize her point, she lifted up the rucksack she had brought with her. The contents clinked and rattled. "Who's going to help me?"

Ellie shook her head slowly. "Tara's right. It's lunacy to fight them. Let's just pray they don't get in here."

Nico glanced across at the window, where Jordan stood chewing away at the last of his baguette. Back at home he didn't seem scared of anything, but since the creatures had appeared he had barely spoken. Behind Jordan, the shutters were open a crack, the sky outside slipping into darkness. It wouldn't be long now until they closed the shutters and started another endless night.

Nico looked back at Hanna. "You told us that the old man said that they're looking for us. That they won't let this storm go until they find us?"

Hanna shrugged. "So he said."

"How can they do that? How can they control the weather? Only Thor can do that and he's not real! It isn't possible."

Tara snorted in his direction. "If you don't have anything more useful to throw in than your expansive knowledge of comic books and geek films, maybe you should leave the talking to the grown-ups."

Nico glared at her, sick of being patronized and belittled by the others. Before he could go back at Tara, Leandra pointed towards the window and the dying light outside. "But the storm's gone now, hasn't it? The wind isn't howling any more, the snowfall's almost stopped."

Tara licked her lips. "Maybe the old man was wrong. Maybe tonight they've gone. Given up."

Nico felt a wave of hope wash over him.

Maybe Hanna was tough enough to smash away at those things in a way Nico could only dream of, but that didn't mean she knew everything. He glanced round at the others. "Maybe she's right! Do you think so?"

Hanna shook her head. "No."

Ellie stood and walked to the shutters. "But look, the storm *has* gone. Leandra's right. Look! Ryan and Shiv could be on their way here, right now, coming to help us!"

Nico saw a flicker of hope on the faces around him, but Hanna was quick to shoot it down. "Or they could be frozen at the edge of a hillside. Or worse."

Tara swore at Hanna and dug her mobile phone out of her pocket. "You don't know that. Ryan will have made it, I know he will. If the storm's gone, help could be on its way right now. They could be here any minute. They might even send a helicopter, right?"

Nico watched as she tapped away at her phone. "Anything?"

"No. There's still no signal. But that doesn't mean anything."

Hanna's eyes never left her. "If this storm has gone, if that old man was talking nothing more than lies, then somebody could make their way up to us. But tomorrow. Not tonight. The pistes will be death-traps with the snow we've had. And there's no way they'd fly a helicopter at night, here in the mountains, not unless it was an emergency. And they don't know what's happening up here."

Nico wiped at his nose. "You're sure?"

Hanna's grey eyes searched him out in the dim light. "Maybe tomorrow. It's been what, three days, since we've had any contact with the valley? That's not unusual. But tomorrow, if this storm stays gone, they might try to send someone up. Maybe. Even if they weren't torn up, the lifts wouldn't run in the winds we've had. But maybe tomorrow somebody will realize things aren't right up here."

Jordan swore and laughed to himself bitterly. "Shit, if they're not here by tomorrow and there's no snow I'm walking down there. No discussion."

Hanna shrugged. "Maybe. But there's no help coming tonight."

The smile slowly seeped from Jordan's face.

"Shit, I'm scared. You know, I've never been

scared of anything before, and I've lost track of the fights I've been in, the times I've been dragged down to the police station. All that stuff, it didn't scare me, not one little bit. But now, right now, I'm shitting it."

Nico stared at him, shocked at Jordan's open admission of fear. But Tara didn't seem to feel a similar sympathy at his revelation.

"Police station? That's awful. You're like, a criminal, aren't you? You're worse than Charlie, even." Tara looked at Jordan as if she was studying some new, rare type of species she hadn't encountered before.

"I never knew anyone before who was in trouble with the law. Now I'm stuck with two of you. But we're all scared. Even the robot girl over there. Although she wouldn't admit it."

Hanna glanced in Tara's direction. "Are you talking about me?"

"If you're not scared you're an idiot, or you're a liar."

Hanna ignored Tara and looked around the group. "I'll tell you what does scare me. What if those things have stopped the storm, the snow? Just turned it off somehow. Think about it. The storm keeps us here but maybe it stops them finding us as well. The wind, the blizzard. Maybe it hinders them hearing us, sensing us. You couldn't see anything out there last night. But now the storm's gone … and they know we can't run, not at night. Not when they're out there."

Tara rolled her eyes in Hanna's direction. "Now you want to believe those … those things control the snow? I thought you didn't believe in monsters and vampires?"

Nico was about to interject another of his film-fuelled observations about creatures that dwelt in the darkness, but Hanna spoke first.

"I still don't. But think about it. Right now, the storm stops. Just as they might be coming out to hunt. Just as they need to see, and hear, and find us."

Nico felt his heart quicken in his chest. "I hope you're wrong."

Hanna walked towards the window, closed the shutter, and turned to face the group. "That old man said they'd find us tonight. I don't want to believe him, but he knew a lot about what's happening here."

All that Nico could see was Hanna's silhouette,

cut out by the pale light of the moon. She let her words sink in, then spoke again. "You can argue with me all you want, but if you want to survive you need to listen to me. I'd rather run. But not if those things are going to hunt me down like a fox and gut me. I don't want to die like that. If they come tonight, we need to make a stand."

Chapter Twenty-nine

Charlie wasn't sure what it was that gave them away.

Just after it had gone dark, Poppy had fallen asleep. She had twisted and turned and moaned in the darkness, mumbling and hissing a stream of gabbled, delirious words. Charlie hadn't been able to understand what it was she was saying, but the sounds alone were haunting.

It had been some time before midnight, Charlie reckoned, when Poppy had woken up and limped off towards the toilet down the hall. A while later, Leandra had switched on the lantern, the light spilling into the room. She'd seemed to check where she was, whispering to herself, then once reassured she'd quickly switched off the light.

Maybe the lantern had given them away, or perhaps it had been Poppy's moans and cries. Or maybe Hanna had been right, and it had only been the storm that had kept them hidden for so long.

At first, the sounds were far off, on the edge of the village, in the forests nearby. Hungry moans, feral cries and shouts, slowly creeping closer to where Charlie and the others lay.

They had taken it in turns to sit at the shutter and peer through the cracks at the frozen world outside. Charlie took the first shift. Just after dark, in the ghostly light of the moon, the still world outside looked almost beautiful. Drifts of snow piled up against the fronts of the chalets and houses opposite the hostel, the pale frosting on the cobbled streets pure and unblemished.

Sitting there, alone, he had almost convinced himself that the last few days had been nothing but a nightmare. But then the howls and cries had drifted to his ears, and he knew that their pursuers were out there, somewhere, on the hunt.

It had been Jordan who took the shift after Charlie. His blocky, battered face had looked pale and drawn, his curly hair silver in the moonlight.

As Charlie passed him the other boy grabbed him by the arm, eyes fixed on the floor as he spoke. "I know I was a dick to you. We was never going to be friends, but you're all right. You could have run for it with Ryan and the others, but you stuck around. So I'm sorry, OK. I just wanted to say that."

Charlie had drifted asleep some time after, wrapped in the folds of his sleeping bag on the hard wooden floor.

He was awake the moment that Jordan's panicked words drifted around the room, the other boy's voice a hushed, strained whisper. "There's two of those things out there. Down by the door. It looks like they're sniffing, like dogs, but I don't think they—"

The sound of splintering wood from downstairs cut Jordan's words dead. Nico bit back a frightened yelp. Charlie opened his eyes and reached for the crowbar that lay next to him. From the speed with which Hanna leaped to her feet he knew that she hadn't been asleep. She picked up her hockey stick and the rucksack that lay inches away from her and hissed at the others.

"They're here, downstairs! Move! Remember what we planned. Go!"

The thin beams of moonlight that shone in through the shutters were more than enough to light the way as the group scrambled up from where they were lying. More sounds came from downstairs, fingers tearing at the wooden shutters, fists pounding the doors.

Leandra grabbed Charlie by the sleeve, her eyes wide and bright. "Are you sure? Are you sure they—"

Hanna pushed her towards the door. "They're here! And if you don't move, you're going to die here. Go!"

Charlie blocked Hanna's way out as she dove for the hallway. "We can still run. We can try to get away from them. I know I said we should fight, but—"

Hanna cut him off before he could finish. "They'll hunt us down. You know they will. You look after the others, I'll try to slow them down here. Take this, then go."

She pressed a small key into his hand, then reached into her bag and brought out a bottle with a rag stuffed into the top. Hanna drew a lighter out of her pocket and glanced up at Charlie. "They'll burn. Everything burns."

After they'd left the old man, Hanna had broken into the small off-licence that sat on Kaldgellen's tiny main street. As she had picked the bottles of spirits off the shelves and passed them to Charlie, he had begun to understand her plan. All of them had fire warnings.

Hanna clicked on the lighter, checking it one last time, then glanced to her right. Jordan stood there, his face ashen and bloodless. "I'm coming with you. I'll help you. If—"

Jordan didn't get to finish his sentence. A piercing scream came from downstairs, high and afraid.

As if thrilled by the sound, the pounding from downstairs intensified, dozens of fists banging on the wood, growls and cries filling the night. Charlie glanced around at the group desperately. "Who is it? Who's down there?"

Nico put his hand up as if he'd suddenly solved a puzzle at school. "Poppy! Where's Poppy?"

Another scream from downstairs, a frantic shout, a word. *Please.*

Tara looked down the stairs fearfully. "We have to leave her! We can't—"

The rest of what she said was lost to Charlie as he ran down the stairs to the source of the screams.

The moon shone through the skylights in the roof

above the derelict reception area. By the pale light Charlie could make out a figure leaning against the wall next to the barricaded front door. As he got closer he could see Poppy's auburn hair. Tears streamed down her cheeks and she seemed to be in a daze.

A long, thin arm slid in through a hole in the wood of the doorway. It lashed around frantically, trying to find a handle or latch to gain entry to the building. Thick, claw-like fingernails scraped patterns on the wood; dirty, bloodstained bandages covering the ravaged flesh of its arm. Charlie reached over to Poppy, put her arm around his neck and half-dragged her to the dusty reception desk in the corner.

"What are you doing down here? What happened?"

Poppy shook her head. "I don't know. I think I was sleepwalking, dreaming. I heard noises, voices in my head, telling me to—"

A huge crash from their left made both of them spin around. Another one of the creatures had started to fight its way into the building, bursting through a boarded-up window. A pale face and half a withered body stuck out into what had once been a long dormitory, rows of rusted bedframes standing by like idle sentries. A few more seconds and the creature would be inside the hostel.

Charlie sprinted into the room, the thing's head whipping in his direction, awful jaws snapping open and shut manically. Tendrils of saliva hung from the intruder's vicious fangs. Charlie was reminded of a set of wind-up teeth he'd had as a child; the ceaseless slam and judder of the dentures as they clicked across the floor.

He rushed at the creature and started to smash away at it with the end of his crowbar. Its dark eyes widened, its attempts to get into the room becoming more and more frantic. Blood ran from its scalp and eyes where Charlie had struck it, but it seemed to barely feel the blows.

Charlie stepped back, lifted the crowbar and swung it as if he was hitting the ball in a game of rounders. He felt the impact judder down his arms, and he watched the creature's jaw sail across the room in a spray of teeth and blood and gore.

Somewhere behind him, Poppy screamed again.

Charlie didn't have time to consider the terror of

the situation or the horror of what he'd just done. Automatically, he pulled the crowbar back once more, slammed it down and felt it dig deep into the creature's skull. The thing jerked convulsively then fell still, its shattered head hanging down over the boarding that covered the window, blood sliding down the plywood sheets.

Charlie turned and ran back towards the hostel's wide reception area. He entered the lobby just as he heard glass shatter somewhere near the doorway. An instant later, the whole room came alive in a flickering dance of flames and a fan of hot air submerged him.

Hanna was over by Poppy, helping her to her feet. Jordan stood by the desk, staring down at his fingers in shock, as if he couldn't quite believe that the flaming bottle had been launched from them. Over by the doorway, the creature that had been trying to get into the lobby whipped this way and that, engulfed in the inferno that had burst out from Jordan's improvised firebomb. The thing was still alive, still trying to get in, but as Charlie watched the flames started to devour its flesh, hair and clothes.

There was a pained, creaking moan from above

and without warning the whole front of the lobby area caved in and fell forwards. As it tumbled inwards, Charlie could see that the weight of several of the creatures had brought the burning door crashing down. They fell on top of the broken panels and the flames leaped from creature to creature then ran along the carpet so that in seconds the whole reception area was ablaze. Despite the heat and smoke, more of the creatures staggered through the door, seeking out their prey.

Charlie glanced at the stairs, started to move before stopping with a lurch. The fire that had spread so quickly from the doorway had created a wall of flame that separated one half of the room from the other.

With growing dread, Charlie realized that he was on one side of the flames and Poppy, Hanna and Jordan were on the other. And there was no way for them to get back up the stairs.

One of the creatures stumbled across the lobby, its hair alight, clawed fingers stretching out of the flames. A green ski jacket covered its upper body, the material spitting and crackling, and for a moment Charlie experienced a jarring flicker of recognition.

It took another step forwards, and Hanna let out a huge roar of rage and fear as she smashed at it with her hockey stick. On the third hit it sank to the ground and lay still.

She spotted Charlie and shouted across at him, struggling to be heard above the roar of the flames. "Go! Back up to the others! We'll meet you! Go!"

Charlie stared at her despairingly but there was no time to argue. As he watched, two more flaming figures staggered into the lobby. Their clothes were burning, their skin melting like wax, their hungry howls and cries twisting into agonized screams.

Hanna's plan, it seemed, was working almost too well.

Somebody called his name from above and Charlie swore loudly and thumped back up the stairs. Smoke was everywhere and by the time he reached the first floor his eyes were streaming, his breath coming in pained gasps.

Nico waited there, his eyes frantic. "Where's Jordan? Where're the others?"

Charlie nodded to his right. "Downstairs. They're cut off. There's dozen of those things, trying to get in, trying to get to us. And the whole lobby's on fire. We need to move!"

Charlie glanced down the stairs one last time, then started to run, along the first-floor corridor, past the empty dorms. A fog of smoke had started to gather near the low ceiling, and Charlie was finding it harder and harder to breathe. He glanced behind him, checked that Nico and the others were there, then scrambled down the stairs at the other end of the corridor, taking them two at a time.

The stairs brought him out at the rear of the building, where a green fire-exit sign showed the way out. There was a door on Charlie's left, boarded up, with a padlock holding it shut on the inside. A terrible symphony of noises came from near the front of the building: shouts, wails, the ravenous roar of flames.

Charlie closed his eyes and tried not to imagine what was going on there. He fished around in his pocket, found the key Hanna had given him earlier and thrust it into the padlock, opening the latch then easing the door open.

Outside, the night was quiet and crisp, layers of snow glistening in the moonlight.

Nico's face appeared next to Charlie's, the bobbles on his orange beanie bouncing around manically atop his head. Behind him, Leandra, Ellie and Tara huddled by the doorway.

Ellie pushed past Nico. "We need to run! Why aren't we running?"

Charlie glanced at the corridor behind them. Smoke billowed from the direction of the lobby, but there was no sign of Hanna and the others.

"We need to wait. I said I'd wait for Hanna."

Leandra dug her fingers into his arm. He resisted the urge to shrug her off. "But she's not here, and those things … if we don't move, they'll find us, won't they?"

Nico stepped towards the doorway, tears glistening in his eyes. "Please. We need to go. Please. We don't know where we're going. If you don't start moving, we're all going to die."

Charlie stared at Nico for a moment, his mind torn. Days before, none of the others had even spoke to him. And now they were looking to him for their safety.

Nothing made sense any more.

Charlie shook his head in a mixture of exasperation, fear and exhaustion, and set out into the night.

Chapter Thirty

Nico was right next to Ellie when the dark, spider-like shape dropped from the rooftop above them and slammed her to the ground.

There hadn't been a time in the past few days when Nico hadn't been scared, and he felt almost exhausted from fear, sick with it. Back home, he spent his evenings battling virtual demons and monsters, but without a controller in his hand and the safety of a screen separating them, the concept was utterly terrifying.

He had barely been able to keep himself moving as they sprinted away from the burning hostel, sure that any moment he'd feel the slash of talons on his back or hear the shriek of a hideous pursuer. But as the crackle of the flames receded in the distance, he had begun to feel a tiny glimmer of hope.

And then one of the grisly creatures had fallen straight into the middle of the group.

Nico's legs tangled up, sending him face first into the snow. He pushed himself up, spat out an icy mouthful and frantically scuttled backwards on his hands and knees, away from their attacker. Glancing to his left, he could see Tara huddled against a wall, eyes screwed closed as if trying to wish herself far away.

The creature rose to its feet, something like a smile on its wide, fanged slit of a mouth. Maybe it was Nico's imagination, but in the moonlight the creature's eyes seemed to shine with glee. It had black, jutting hair, and a ragged bandage ran around its head, across one eye, dirty brown marks staining the gauze.

It opened its mouth as if to let loose a roar of triumph. Before it could get the sound out, the end of Charlie's crowbar smashed it across the brow.

Their assailant's head snapped back and it staggered drunkenly. A thin line of blood ran down from its raven hair, trickling on to the snow. Its limbs writhed around as it stumbled, the claws at the end of its bloated fingers slashing blindly. Leandra cried out and fell backwards. Charlie ducked this way and that, as if he were a boxer, trying to thrust his crowbar at their attacker a second time.

Nico's back hit the alleyway wall just as Charlie found an opening. The metal bar thundered straight down on to the top of the creature's head. Its legs folded under the blow, the top of its skull caving in. A glut of blood spattered across the snow.

"Come on, we need to move, if the others have heard—"

Charlie's words choked as his eyes fell upon Leandra.

She sat deadly still a few feet from Nico, a widening pool of blood colouring the snow around her. Where the creature's talons had ripped out Leandra's throat, a crimson slick pulsed out in steady throbs and ran down the front of her orange puffer jacket.

She couldn't speak, but her eyes said it all. They were wide with terror and disbelief, and Nico watched as the light in the pupils trickled away. Nobody uttered a sound as Leandra crumpled next to her killer. Wide-eyed, Charlie stepped over the creature's body and tried to pull Leandra to her feet.

Ellie staggered up and put her hand on his shoulder. Her words were gentle, soft. "She's gone Charlie. She's dead. We have to leave her here."

Charlie's lips parted, but no words came out. He looked at Leandra's motionless form then glanced back at Ellie. "Dead?"

Ellie nodded slowly.

Charlie wiped his eyes numbly and let Leandra sink back down on to the snow.

There were more noises, cries and shouts, growing closer. Nico looked back the way they had come and only just fought the urge to run blindly into the darkness beyond. He turned towards Charlie, desperate now, his voice breaking as he pleaded. "We need to go. We can't help her, Charlie. Please!"

Charlie took a last look at Leandra's serene face, and turned back to the group, wondering if any of them would live to see the dawn.

Chapter Thirty-one

"What is this place? Is he dead?"

Someone gasped and Nico took a cautious step away from the figure slumped in the chair.

Charlie ignored Nico's question and tried the handle on the heavy wooden cellar door. In the dim light, he could just make out a series of stone steps leading downwards. He took a torch out of his pocket and shone it into the space below. It revealed two wooden racks against a stone wall, a mattress on the other side of the cellar.

He turned back to the others. "That's the old man we told you about. And yeah, he's dead. If he wasn't, he'd be down there, hiding from those things."

Tara took a step closer to the chair and stuck up her nose. "I can't stay here. I can't stay next to him."

Charlie glanced towards the huge bay window and closed his eyes while he tried to calm himself. They were moments from being discovered, Hanna and the others were missing, most likely dead, but Tara's focus was still squarely on herself.

Once he had himself sufficiently under control as to not bellow at her, he turned in Tara's direction. "You don't have to. There's a wine cellar down there and this door locks from the inside. If you're quiet and lucky, you'll be safe."

Nico stared at him. "Why do you keep saying *you*? Why not *we*?"

"I need to go back out. I need to hide our tracks, or make some more. Our footsteps lead right here. I don't know how clever those things are, but if they've got half a brain they could probably track us down in minutes."

Ellie shook her head. "Seriously? You're going to go back out there? With those things running around?"

Charlie passed his torch to Nico. "You think I want to? You really think I want to go out there and risk my neck for all of you? But how safe do you think we'll be if they work out we're here? And how long do you think that door will hold them?"

Nobody spoke. Nico took a hesitant look at Charlie, then cautiously made his way down into the darkness, Tara behind him.

Ellie paused, looked at the front door then grabbed Charlie's arm. "You can't do this on your own. I'm coming with you."

Charlie felt a flicker of gratitude at her words, and he pushed the door shut behind Tara. He waited for the sound of the latch clicking into place before they left the chalet.

Outside, the sky of the village was lit by an orange glow that illuminated the mountains all around, sparks and smoke dancing up joyfully into the air. Charlie glanced around, but there was still no sign of Hanna and the others.

He watched the sepia light flicker on the snow for a moment, then nodded at Ellie and led her away into the night.

Chapter Thirty-two

Charlie and Ellie made it back to the chalet just as the heavens started to lighten, both of them exhausted and scared. They had spent most of the night hiding in the shadows, trying to cover the tracks they had made on the way to the old man's home, scrambling almost blindly through the dark as they made false trails.

As the night had slipped towards dawn, they had made their way as close to the hostel as they dared, sheltering in a doorway that gave them a clear view of the carnage. The derelict building had burned and raged, the upper floors collapsing in on themselves like dominoes, the dull rumble echoing away into the night. There had been no sign of Hanna, Poppy or Jordan. Every now and then, amidst the smoke, quick figures darted near the flames, searching, hunting. When one of the shapes had glanced in their direction, Ellie swore in fright, and for a heartbeat Charlie thought they had been discovered.

Finally they had slipped back to the old man's chalet, locked the door and made a nest of cushions and blankets next to the huge bay window. A pale light had just started to shimmer along the edge of the mountains, tracing the edges of the land far away.

Wolfgang's body still sat there in the chair in the middle of the lounge, slowly decomposing, but neither of them had the strength to care. While Ellie closed her eyes on an old sofa, Charlie huddled and shivered under a prickly blanket, and fell into a deep, exhausted sleep.

The creak of the cellar door dragged Charlie from vague dreams, Hanna's face never far away. A moment later Tara and Nico crept into the dining room, grumbling about aches and pains and the cold, their breath fogging about them as they spoke. For a moment Charlie wanted nothing more than to keep his eyes closed, to avoid having to re-emerge into this nightmare world where death was seconds away and strangers relied on him to keep them alive.

But he knew he would only be delaying the inevitable.

Nobody remarked on the body that sat in the middle of the room, its horror now a strange shared normality. The four of them ate a breakfast of cheese and milk from remnants left in the old man's fridge, then Charlie rose wearily to his feet.

"I need to go. I need to check the hostel for the others. I need to make sure."

Nico nodded, his eyes drifting to the still figure that slumped in the chair like a drunkard. "I don't want to stay here. I'll come with you."

The girls nodded their assent, but Tara stopped them at the front door. "You're sure? You're sure those things won't—"

Charlie gave an exhausted nod. "They don't come out in the day. I think we're pretty sure of that now."

"Vampires," whispered Nico to no one in particular. This time none of them bothered to argue with him.

They emerged from the chalet into the grey light of day, eyes blinking from smoke and long hours shut in the dark.

They were silent as they stumbled into the

morning air, but Charlie was sure they'd all noticed that the snow had started to fall again, the wind slowly rising in a whistling accompaniment. Dawn had brought a clear, pale sky the colour of steel, but minute by minute more clouds slipped in from the west.

Nobody shut the front door, the thin wood left to slam against the frame in the breeze.

Before he realized where he was, Charlie's footsteps took them past the spot where they had been attacked the night before. Blood stained the snow, faintly masked now by fresh powder. But both Leandra's body and that of her attacker were gone.

Nico stood and stared at the spot. His mumbled words echoed away down the deserted alleyway. "What if there's just us four left now?"

He started crying, pressing a shaking hand over his mouth to quieten the sobs.

Charlie turned away and they set off to the hostel. As they crept closer, the smell of smoke became more and more pungent, until the air was heavy with it. A low mist lingered in the village streets, the growing wind doing little to banish it. Navigating the gloom, they rounded the corner to what was left of the derelict hostel.

It was a while before any of them spoke, each lost in their own thoughts, mesmerized by the wreckage beyond.

The whole front of the hostel was now a charred, fuming pile of logs and beams, the rest of the building stripped away so that there was little more left than a blackened, twisted carcass. The snow had started to fall more heavily now, and from the skeletal debris came the hiss and fizz of flakes as they found their way down on to the smouldering ruins.

Charlie took a deep breath and started towards the ashes.

"Where are you going?" asked Tara.

Charlie ignored the question and made his way over to where the front of the building had stood only hours before. The drifts around his feet melted away as he got nearer to the hostel, and fragments of wood and glass and twisted metal littered the ground.

His dread only grew as he stepped over the remains of the boarded-up front door that had caved in the night before. A charred, bony hand poked out from underneath the burnt planks. Charlie peered down, then moved away when he saw the long talons that protruded from the ends of the fingers.

There were more bodies in the ruins of the lobby, a pitiful litter of charred bones, fragments of clothing and ragged bandages. He peered at one skull, split like a melon with a wide, leering grin, the teeth long and serrated. Charlie's mind replayed the sounds of the night before, the screams and the cries and roaring flames, and he couldn't help but think of the moment he had last seen Hanna, staring back at him amidst the growing inferno.

A crunch from the entrance made him spin round. Nico was there, his face almost sapped of colour, his eyes wide and fraught. Ellie and Tara huddled behind, their eyes flicking left and right.

"Was Hanna ever right," Nico whispered. "Those things burn."

From above them, the stripped corpse of the upper floors creaked and groaned, and a lazy rain of melted snow descended on the ashen ruin.

Charlie's heart jerked as his eyes spotted something in the snow. He crept over, swore, and then kneeled down next to a charred, blackened body.

"What is it?"

Charlie didn't reply to Nico's words. Instead, he reached down into the rubble, drawing out a long, thin, curved piece of metal from where it lay partly hidden.

Hanna's hockey stick.

"Oh no," whispered Nico, moving closer and looking down at the body. "Is that...?"

Charlie stared at the grisly find. The skin and hair and clothes had burned away, so that all remained was a collection of bones and ash, a skull atop them like the point of an exclamation mark. He reached out and touched the jawline.

Tara's whispered words drifted amidst the fog. "It's her, isn't it? It's Hanna."

Charlie glanced up at Nico. His voice started to break as he spoke. "We can't leave her here. We need to get a spade, bury her. We need to—"

A noise from the doorway made everyone jerk and turn. Tara yelped like a dog and leaped behind what was left of the charred desk.

There was a cough, the shuffle of feet, and a

dishevelled, blackened figure stumbled unsteadily into the room.

Hanna took another step, blinked at the light, then brushed soot and dirt from her eyes with her sleeve. There was a long, thin scratch down one side of her face, and her black hair was speckled with a frosting of ash. The knuckles on one hand were ripped and torn and her other hand was wrapped in a bloody piece of cloth.

Charlie wrestled against a powerful urge to run over to Hanna, to throw his arms around her and hold her tight. He blinked back tears, and when he spoke his voice felt hoarse and shaky. "How? How did you stay alive?"

Hanna made her way towards Charlie and stared down at the charred skeleton by his boots. She wiped at her nose with the bloody bandage that covered her fingers.

"This one kept us alive. Jordan. He held them back so I could get Poppy clear. He said he'd follow us. But he didn't. He kept them back instead."

Tara stared at Hanna. "Did Poppy…?"

Hanna gestured at the row of shops on the other side of the square. "She's alive. Just about. She was asleep when I left her. Asleep and delirious."

Charlie stood up and offered the hockey stick to Hanna. She stared at it for a moment then took it off him.

"How did you get out?"

Hanna looked back down at Jordan's scorched remains. "After you ran, after I sent you back to the others, more of those things got in. They were on fire by the time they got near to us, frantic, screaming, running this way and that. Poppy couldn't walk, so Jordan shouted at me to carry her away while he held them off. He said he'd be right behind us. But when I looked back I saw him, standing there, a stream of them coming at him. And then I saw the roof fall in, right on top of it all."

Nico shook his head. "I never liked him. He scared me. He used to bully me in school. I can't believe he gave his life for us."

Charlie's mind slipped back to their conversation just hours before. "How did you get out of the hostel?"

There's a window down there, one that wasn't boarded up. One of those things got there first. Jordan had my stick, so I used a burning piece of wood to get it out of our way. I wish I hadn't."

Hanna held up her right hand, the fingers red and seared. She winced and lowered her arm.

"We clambered out of the window, made it outside. The fire was so bad that the smoke hid us from them. I managed to drag Poppy over to the butcher's store and we shut ourselves in the storage locker, down in the basement. Poppy slept, but I couldn't. The door wouldn't bolt, so I just sat there, holding it closed, waiting for them."

She looked up at the sky that glowered down through the open ceiling. "It's snowing again, isn't it? I don't think we're getting off this mountain. Not ever. Where's the other girl? Leandra?"

Charlie glanced at the others then shook his head.

Hanna nodded slowly, caught a flake of snow on her open palm and watched it melt away on her skin. "Yesterday I thought we had a chance. Now I'm not so sure. There were dozens of those things last night. We killed a few. But there are less of us every day. We can hide again, try to barricade the doors, the windows. But they'll find us. We're all exhausted. Injured. Nobody's coming to help, not today, not with this weather.

We can't keep doing this."

Charlie stared at her in disbelief. "So what? Give up?"

Hanna looked up from the droplet of water on her palm and met his eyes.

"No. I'm going to fight for as long as I can. But I don't think any of us are getting away from Kaldgellan. I think we need to face up to that."

Nico pointed at the shoulder of one of the mountains nearby. "What's that place up there? I've wondered since the first day. Is that a cross?"

A mixture of smoke and low mist obscured the view, but Charlie could just make out a small grey building on the edge of the trees.

Hanna nodded without interest and picked at the cut on the side of her face. Charlie didn't want to ask her how she'd got it. Hanna stifled a yawn and looked away into the distance.

"It's an old church. They close it in the winter, but in the summer they have weddings there, christenings. If you're hoping for help, there's not going to be anyone there."

Nico continued to stare up at the church. He turned towards the rest of the group. "If I'm going to die, I want to do it next to God. I'm going to head up there. I don't want to go on my own, but I don't want to stay down here any more either. Does anyone want to come with me?"

Hanna glanced around at the rest of the group. Ellie shrugged, the golden hoops in her ears jiggling with the motion. "Why not?"

Charlie nodded, and felt a wave of resignation wash away a little of the fear he felt. "Let's do it. It's as good a place to hide as any."

Hanna raised her eyebrows. For a heartbeat Charlie thought she might shoot down the idea, but instead she nodded slowly. When she spoke again, she seemed more alert, as if the sudden sense of purpose had snapped her out of her stupor.

"If we're going to get up there, with your friend Poppy in the state she's in, we need to get moving. It's not far, and there's a path that will get us up there, but with this snow it might still take us a while. So if we're going to do it, let's get started."

Chapter Thirty-three

The climb was far harder than it looked.

From among the blackened beams of the hostel, Hanna had reckoned it would take little more than an hour or two's brisk march. But between the biting wind, the deep pillows of snow and Poppy's bite wound, it was taking them far longer.

Hanna had only let them pack the most basic of supplies to take up to the chapel. Sleeping bags. A few tins of food from the village stores. A torch each. She'd suspected that they wouldn't be staying in the church long, one way or another.

As they trudged through the deep banks of snow, Hanna fiddled with the bandage on her hand, trying her best to forget the events of the night before.

Fighting hadn't worked.

She was more than lucky to still be alive. But worse was the fact that Jordan had given his life to save her and Poppy. As was the knowledge that, had their positions been reversed, Hanna would have left him to die without a backwards glance.

Somehow, that awareness hurt her more than the cuts and the burns and the bruises. Through a sea of aches and pains, Hanna wondered absently if what she had become to obtain her revenge would leave her in a place of absolution, or condemned forever. As the cold slowly seeped into her bones, she realized that there was no easy answer.

They assumed by now that they were safe in the daylight, but all the same none of them wanted to be alone or to stray too from the group. Charlie and Nico walked on either side of Poppy, supporting her up the slopes, but Tara had her phone in her hand, her eyes locked on to its screen. Her fingers weren't moving, but her eyes never left the small, neat rectangle. Despite herself, Hanna found her feet dragging her closer.

"Anything?"

Tara continued to study the phone in her still, pale fingers. "My battery's gone. I haven't had any signal for days, but at least I could look at it, check it. Now it's gone."

Tara shook her head mournfully and threw her

phone away. It landed in a deep drift of snow and sank out of view. "Maybe somebody will find it, one day. There are texts that wouldn't send, stuck in the outbox. Maybe somebody will find it and know what really happened to us up here."

Hanna stole a glance at Poppy, whose glassy eyes were lingering on the bandage around her ankle. Maybe it was Hanna's imagination, but Poppy's auburn hair seemed somehow thinner and her face seemed to have a yellowed, pallid sheen. There were black lines under her eyes and a prickle of sweat stood out on her skin, despite the cold. She had been delirious in the night, thrashing about as if possessed and muttering the strangest of words. The wound on her leg had begun to stink, a sickly, sweet odour, and Hanna wasn't sure how long Poppy had left without some serious medical attention.

Hanna rubbed at her grainy eyes, brushed the snow away from her face and looked around at the group.

"You still sure about this?"

Nico nodded. "My mum always made me go to church. My dad's family were from the Congo, but Mum's Irish-Italian and she insisted they raise me

261

Catholic. With a name like Nicolino, I guess that's no surprise, huh? But yeah, I'm still sure."

By the time they made their way on to the drifts that covered the chapel's wide driveway, the dull glimmer of light that had somehow made it through the thick clouds was beginning to fade away. The snow was heavier now, the cold wind a constant moan. A low rumble echoed from the way they had come, and Charlie paused and looked back.

"Thunder?"

Hanna stopped alongside him and shook her head. "Avalanche. Further down the valley. That will make any snow patrols that were planning to head up this way think twice."

Hanna took one last look down at Kaldgellan. A deathly layer of cloud, smoke and mist hung over the empty streets. Hanna could just make out the charred ruin of the hostel on one side of the village, the front of the minibus jutting out of the ruined ski shop. Charlie stepped alongside her, leaving Poppy with Nico.

"You think some of them are still down there? The locals, hiding, waiting?"

Hanna scanned the village for any sign of

movement. "I don't know. If they are, I hope they freeze to death."

Charlie blew out a misty breath. "If that old man was right, if the people here hide the truth about those things, what story will they use to explain this away? How will they cover it up?"

Ellie chewed at a frayed fingernail. "Maybe we'll be here to tell them the truth. Maybe those things wont find us up here."

Poppy coughed − a bloody, raw sound, and Charlie lifted her up and set off again. A dozen more footsteps and the chapel slid into view. Yellowing chunks of worn stone made up the walls, covered in places by thick moss. Behind the chapel a wall of frosted pines bled into thick forest. Hanna found herself wondering how good an idea this was, and what might be lying further into the trees, amidst the shadows and the darkness.

An old oak door blocked their path, worn, weather−beaten, decorated with faded iron studs. Hanna stared at it for a moment, then turned the solid metal knocker and heaved the door inwards. The chapel wasn't locked and a breath of stale air seeped out of the darkness.

Ellie was next to Hanna. "What if something's in there? Are you sure we should—"

Before she could finish her sentence Hanna pulled a torch out of her pocket, clicked it on and slid through the gap in the doorway. Ellie hesitated before following her, and once the others were in Charlie helped Poppy through the door.

Shafts of dim daylight filtered in from stained-glass windows up near the high ceiling, revealing the interior of the chapel. Rows of wooden benches led from the doorway to a curved archway at the end and a small chamber beyond. There was an aisle between the two rows of benches and the others wandered behind Hanna past the empty wooden seats.

Even with the high windows, the church was swamped in darkness and shadow. Hanna's torch flicked this way and that like the spotlight of a police helicopter, the beam swimming with dust. The bitter air of the chapel was almost as numbing as the wind outside, but all the same it was a relief to be out of the storm and snow.

Charlie lowered Poppy on to a bench near the doorway. She shivered, lay down and curled into a ball on her side, closing her eyes. Hanna watched her for a moment then shuffled further inside. The high ceiling amplified their voices and their breathing, the sound of their boots.

The others waited by the altar while Charlie investigated the small doorway that led off to the right. Hanna felt so tired she could barely stand and she leaned on the altar to keep from falling over.

Tara glanced at the small lectern that looked out over the rows of benches. "People got married here, didn't they? Happy couples, people in love, people excited about the rest of their lives. Do you think they knew that … knew about those things out there?"

Ellie pulled her furry hood down from her face and wiped a finger of dust from the Bible that lay on the lectern. "I hope not. I think if people knew, if good people knew, they'd tell the world, wouldn't they?" Ellie looked around at the others for some kind of reassurance.

Hanna shook her head slowly. "That old man we found was happy enough to keep those things a secret, so long as he kept his own skin safe. Some people will do anything to keep themselves alive, no matter how terrible it might seem."

Charlie walked back to the others and stared out at the rows of empty seats. Nico nodded towards the room off to the right. "What's in there?"

"Not much. A small changing room and a toilet. A rail full of robes. Candles, a few bottles of wine and some cups, and a corridor that leads away to a locked door at the back of the chapel. Nobody's getting through that, not without a battering ram."

Tara watched as her breath unfurled into the darkness and shot an angry look in Nico's direction. "It's like a freezer in here. It's colder than outside. I wanted somewhere to hide, not a place to freeze to death."

Hanna just managed to scrape together the strength to come back at the other girl. "It might be cold, but it's as safe as anywhere. Nobody would be able to get up to those windows, they're too high. That door at the front is solid, and we can bolt it from the inside."

Ellie looked across at Hanna hopefully. "You think we'll be safe?"

Hanna's eyes lingered on the door at the far end of the chapel. "If those things find us, it's going to

take them a long time to break through that door.
We might have a chance, just as long as they don't
find us any time soon."

Chapter Thirty-four

As dusk approached they set up a small camp near the front of the chapel, as far away from the door as it was possible to get.

Only adrenaline was keeping Charlie standing as he lit half a dozen of the candles from the side room and placed them around the altar area, so that the sleeping bags basked in a warming, orange glow. The wind still whined and howled, but the chapel felt less frigid with the bodies that now occupied it.

Poppy had been asleep for most of the afternoon and she barely stirred when Nico leaned across to offer her some food.

"Leave her," whispered Hanna. "Let her rest."

Nico nodded and passed the backpack full of food to the others. Charlie stared at the bag for a moment before taking a tin of ravioli. He pulled the lid off the tin and reluctantly munched away at the chilled contents.

Outside, a harsh gust of wind rattled the windows in the ceiling. Daylight was almost gone now, the shadows in the chapel growing deeper by the minute. All of them sat wrapped in their coats, clothes and sleeping bags. In other circumstances, Charlie thought, it could have made for a perfect teenage sleepover or camping trip. Except those he found himself trapped with would never have acknowledged him, if not for what had happened.

He finished his food, put the can to one side, then closed his eyes and leaned back against the stone wall. He had barely slept the night before and within seconds he started to feel himself dozing. A muffled crash from somewhere outside jerked him awake.

Hanna's face was just across from his inside the circle of light, her grey eyes alert and awake. "Just a branch, blown down by the wind. Go back to sleep."

Black strands of her hair hung down like snakes from her scalp and the cut on the side of her face looked raised and angry.

"You sure it's not them?" whispered Nico. His voice was unsteady, and even in the gloom Charlie could see him shaking.

"We'll know soon enough," hissed Hanna.

For a while no one spoke, then Nico sat up, pulled down the Bible from the lectern and placed it next to him.

"Maybe God will look after us. Maybe he'll keep us safe."

Hanna shook her head slowly, the strands of her hair dancing in the candlelight. "I doubt it. I don't believe there's a God. Or heaven. Or hell. Just people."

Tara stared across at Hanna, her sleeping bag pulled up under her chin. "What are those things, then? They're not people, that's for sure."

Hanna shrugged. "I don't know. But whatever they are, nobody is watching over us."

Tara leaned her head to one side, blond hair catching in the ochre light. "Then why were you so keen to come here?"

Hanna played with the bandage around her hand, picking at the scabs on her fingers. "It's high. It's secure. And it's just as good a place to die as any."

In the corner, Poppy suddenly wailed and cried, her voice high and frantic. "They're coming. They know we're here. She sees us, she…"

Ellie and Nico gasped in fright at the sudden noise and Tara wriggled away in her sleeping bag. Even Hanna's face looked tight with fear. She peered closer, leaning over Poppy.

"It's OK, she's asleep now, she—"

Poppy's arm darted up, her fingers grabbing the hood of Hanna's coat. Hanna swore and jerked away. Poppy sat up and looked around, her eyes delirious and unseeing.

"They're alive, please, some of them are still alive … and the others, they've changed, they've…"

Poppy moaned and started to cry. Ellie wrapped an arm around her, pulling her close. "Shhh. It's OK, it's all right. Shhh."

Ellie glanced up at the others. "She's on fire… Her skin… She's burning up."

Hanna studied Poppy's face, then leaned closer once more and touched Poppy's shoulder. "Who, Poppy? Who's alive?"

"Stefan. Stefan and Kelsey and Malachi and… Oh God, no, I can see them, she has them, she's making them … making them…"

Charlie was on his knees staring across at Poppy. His mouth was dry, his heart pounding in his chest as if it were about to rip out of his ribs. When he spoke, his words were like sawdust in his mouth. "She's dreaming, she's just—"

Hanna held up her open palm to silence Charlie. She leaned closer still to Poppy's sweating face. "Where? Where are they?"

Poppy shook her head and squinted at the doorway at the far end of the church. "In the caves. In the caves, by the hidden trail. Where the rocks are kissed by diamonds. She lets me see sometimes. But she's coming, she's going to get in, she won't come through the door, but ... but..."

Poppy's words stopped and she started to sob uncontrollably again. She nestled next to Ellie for a few seconds, then sat up and wiped at her eyes, glancing around at the shadowed faces.

"Where am I? Where..."

Ellie stroked Poppy's hair and held her close. "You're safe, you're OK. You were just dreaming. You're going home soon. Go back to sleep now."

Poppy nodded groggily. Her voice was hoarse, her words a dry, tiny whisper. "I've been having the worst dreams, terrible dreams. Voices in my head, screaming at me. And my ankle it..."

She made as if to reach down to her wounded leg, but the energy seemed to ebb away from her. Her eyes closed and she slipped down next to Ellie.

For a long time nobody spoke. Charlie counted the minutes as his heartbeat slowly calmed.

Ellie eased away from Poppy, laying her head down to rest on the bed of cushions that they had taken from the wooden benches that lined the church. She sighed and looked imploringly up at the others. "What the hell was that? She was dreaming, wasn't she?"

Tara nodded. "She had to be. She had to."

Charlie glanced across at Hanna. There was a look on her face that he couldn't read, something between fear and incomprehension. He stared at her, a cold certainty forming in his mind.

"You know, don't you? The caves she talked about, you know where they are, don't you?"

Hanna wouldn't meet his eyes. Instead, she picked at the cut on the side of her face. "Maybe. There's a run, not too far from here. It takes you past a sheer a cliff-face. But there's a crack in the stone, a gap, and you can cut through it, duck down, and the rock there, it's peppered with shining stones. Diamonds, the villagers used to call them. And in the rock-face nearby, there's a series of caves. I've never been in — they're far from safe — but I've seen them. But there's no way Poppy could know about that place. Only the locals know. Only the people who live on the mountain know where she's talking about. She couldn't."

Nico swore. The tone of his voice was several rungs above the edge of panic. "Then how can she know? How can she?"

Hanna's voice betrayed a tiny edge of uncertainty. "How should I know? Maybe she ... maybe she read about it on the internet? Maybe a friend of hers had been here, had ... I don't know! It doesn't make sense!"

Hanna glanced across at Poppy. "She's dying. I sat with her last night, I looked at her ankle and it's turned bad. Gangrenous. It's enough to make anybody feverish. Without a doctor, without a hospital, she's not going to last another day."

She reached across, dug into a pocket of her backpack and pulled out a roll of medical gauze and a pair of scissors. "If she's still with us in the morning, we'll bandage it again. For all the good it will do."

Tara looked up at the windows above their head. The sky was dark now, the moon all but hidden by a thick layer of clouds. "We can't do anything, can we? There's nothing we can do to help her. I don't know her, not really. But it could be me lying there, couldn't it, instead of her?"

Across from Charlie, Ellie leaned forwards, a terrified sheen in her eyes. "Poppy said they were still alive, didn't she. *Changing*. I didn't want to tell anyone this, but ... last night I saw something. When I was with Charlie, after you went into the basement. One of those things, at the hostel. It looked just like Malachi. I mean, it can't have been. But it looked just like him."

Charlie felt a cold dread prickle his skin, a flashback to the flaming hostel playing in his mind. He'd recognized one of the creatures, just as it caught fire. He'd seen its face before, sitting two rows behind him on the coach as they set off for Austria.

A horrified look swam across Tara's face, but before she could start to speak Nico beat her to it.

"Vampires can turn humans. Like in *Salem's Lot*. *Blade*. *Near Dark*. That's what they do. That's how they make others."

Tara leaned in Nico's direction, a step away from hysterics. "What does that even mean?"

Nico wiped at his eyes. "Maybe it means that if they take you, they make you just like them. Maybe that's why they dragged away the bodies of the other students, that first night at the hotel. "

Tara shook her head, her voice rising, panicked. "I'm not talking about all that fantasy nonsense you and your geek friends nerd out over! What about the fact she saw Malachi? Does it mean that those things caught Malachi and Shiv? That they caught Ryan? That he's … he's…"

Ellie reached across and put her hand on Tara's. "I don't know what I saw. It was dark, smoky. Maybe it was just my imagination. Maybe I was just exhausted."

Ellie's words seemed to calm Tara down, averting the screams that seemed on the verge of echoing around the chapel. Charlie decided it was best not to share what he had seen that night, and he felt a short-lived wave of relief when Tara sat back, her face haunted.

It was a while before anyone else spoke, Ellie's admission rendering the group stunned and silent. A small silver chain hung around Tara's neck, a crucifix, and Charlie watched her lift it out from under her top and study it.

"Will those ... will those things find us here?"

Hanna shrugged. Tara's eyes drifted towards the heavy wooden door at the front of the chapel.

Nico wiped tears away from his cheeks, then lay back on his sleeping bag. Hanna sat and stared at Poppy, her bandaged fingers on the handle of her hockey stick.

For a while, the only sound was the wind moaning around the eaves. Charlie started to wonder if the rest of the group had gone to sleep, until Nico's voice abruptly echoed out of the gloom. "I don't want to die. I mean, there's so much I never did. I never travelled. This is the furthest I've ever been from home. I never got to go to America, I always wanted to go there, go to Comic Con. I never got to see how *Game of Thrones* ended. It might sound stupid, but it meant a lot to me. And I never even got the chance to, I mean I never had a girlfriend, so I never got to…"

Hanna glanced across at him. "Have sex?"

He nodded slowly. Even by the candlelight Charlie could tell Nico was embarrassed.

Hanna stared at him. "You want to know what it's like?"

Nico's eyes widened. "No! I mean, not like—"

Tara snorted and Hanna shook her head. "Don't flatter yourself. I'm not going to do it with you. I meant, do you want me to *tell* you what it's like?"

Nico put his head in his hands. "I'm such a loser," he mumbled.

Charlie looked across at him and shook his head. "Doesn't matter. I've never done it either. So if you're a loser, I'm a loser, too."

Hanna stared at him and raised her eyebrows. "I'm sorry. That day when I walked in on you with that pretty dark-haired girl, Leandra… If I hadn't disturbed you, perhaps you would have had the chance."

Charlie shook his head. "Don't worry. I'm pretty sure that I would have been too scared to … you know."

Nico glanced across at Hanna. "So what … what is it like?"

Hanna shrugged. "It's nothing special. It's supposed to be good with the right person. Better, anyway. Too bad I never found the right person to try out that theory."

Maybe it was Charlie's imagination, maybe it was the light, but Hanna's gaze seemed to linger on him, studying him. He felt a nervous twinge in his gut as he caught her eye and she quickly looked away.

On the other side of the altar, Tara sniffed. "I did, I think. I found my right person. But I don't think I'm going to see him again."

Ellie leaned her head to one side. "Ryan?"

Tara nodded. "It was never going to work, was it? As soon as my mum found out where he lived, she'd have grounded me until I agreed to stop seeing him. He made me a better person, I think. He always made me feel special."

She stared at the pendant in her fingers and then glanced at the heavy wooden door at the other end of the chapel once more, as if trying to cling on to the dream that Ryan might burst in through it at any second with a rescue party.

Tara's bottom lip wobbled, the hope slowly draining from her eyes. "He's not coming, is he? Maybe Ellie wasn't imagining it. I'm not going to see Ryan again, am I?"

Hanna dipped a finger into the line of candlewax that slid down from one of the flames. She glanced across at Tara and picked the drying coating from her fingertip. "Honestly? It doesn't look good."

Chapter Thirty-five

They came in the dead of night, when even the most anxious of the group was asleep. Charlie had been drifting through feverish, colour-bleached dreams, back in the frozen Scottish highlands with his dad.

Then the noises had begun.

The hammering seemed to start all at once, from every corner of the walls. A cacophony of banging fists, howls, shouts and scratching fingernails.

Ellie scrambled to her feet before Charlie's eyes were even fully open. Her voice was high with panic. "Shit, they've found us, what do we do? Where do we go?"

"Quiet, everyone, quiet!" Hanna hissed.

Charlie's mouth was dry, but he didn't feel scared. Instead, he felt a numb finality wash over him, a strange sense of calm. He curled his fingers around the crowbar and turned to Hanna. "This is it, isn't it? There's nowhere to run this time."

Hanna swore. "They're at the front and the back. The two places they could find a way in. They should hold. But we need to make sure they don't get in, or we're finished. Nico, I need you and Tara to go to the back door. It's chained shut and the wood is heavy, but we need to be sure."

Nico didn't move. He put his hands to his mouth and shook his head. There were tears in his eyes.

Tara's eyes were wide and frantic. "I don't want to die. I don't want those things to get me, make me one of them! *Please*."

Charlie sighed and licked sandpaper lips. "I'll go. I'll guard it. You look after the front door."

Hanna nodded and lifted her backpack. A clink of glass came from inside the bag, the last of the alcohol that had started the terrible blaze at the hostel. Outside, the clamouring and hammering seemed to notch up a level, so that Charlie almost had to shout to be heard. "If we burn them, if we use the bottles, there's no way out. The fire spreads and we'll burn in here."

Hanna's eyes were flat, her voice steady and resigned. "Better that than turn into one of those things."

She turned towards the front door. The old wood jerked and jumped with a multitude of impacts, and Charlie imagined the horde outside, scratching and beating to gain entry. Ellie backed away until she thudded into the wall. "How many are there?"

Charlie met Hanna's eyes. "If they get in, run for the back door. We can fight our way out there."

Charlie knew it was a lie, but he said it anyway. He was amazed at how steady his voice sounded, how little fear he felt. Hanna seemed on the verge of saying something, and her eyes lingered on Charlie. Instead she nodded, dropped her coat and rucksack, clutched her hockey stick and made her way to the front doors.

Charlie watched her go and wondered if this might be the last time he would see her. Then he gripped the crowbar between his slippery fingers, turned, and started to run to the rear of the chapel.

Chapter Thirty-six

Hanna took slow, hesitant steps towards the chapel door. It took all she had not to just turn, run and hide, close her eyes and wait for the inevitable.

But somehow she kept walking.

There was a scream from somewhere behind her. Hanna ignored it and took another step. She gripped the battered hockey stick tightly and held it in front of her like a talisman, her burnt fingers throbbing and complaining. While the others had slept, she had entertained the thought that perhaps the creatures wouldn't find them.

Now she knew otherwise.

Perhaps they had followed their tracks. Or perhaps they had smelled them on the wind. Whatever it was, they were here now, and they wanted to get inside.

As she crept closer, the battered wooden door came more and more into focus. Hanna could see that the thick oak held firm. It juddered and shifted, but there were no cracks in the wood, no talons or fingers poking through. For now, the door was keeping them out.

Hanna lowered the hockey stick, her breath coming in short gasps. She was just about to turn around when the noise from the other side of the door ceased.

It was as if someone outside had turned off a switch, or as if whatever was creating the riot of sound had suddenly, instantly, fallen asleep. For a heartbeat there was absolute silence in the dim light of the chapel, no sound in Hanna's ears except the pounding of her heart.

Hanna stared at the door, confused.

As her hockey stick slipped down to her side two words broke the silence.

"Hello, pretty."

The sudden, foreign voice made the hairs on Hanna's arms stand up. It was as if a cold blast of air had blown straight through the back wall of the chapel and on to her exposed skin.

She started to turn, knowing she was a fraction too late, knowing that the breath from the words had been at her neck.

There was a deep, piercing pain across her bicep. Hanna cried out and felt her hockey stick drop from her numb fingers.

A bright shimmer of steel slashed for her face and she took two quick instinctive steps backwards.

A figure stood in front of her, long auburn hair curled around a pale face, a mocking smile on her lips. Its bloodied fingers held a pair of scissors, the curved blade brandished forwards like a knife. The figure took an unsteady step and Hanna saw that one of its feet was bandaged and bloody, the ankle swollen and ravaged.

Hanna took another step backwards. "You're…"

The dreadful smile grew wider. "Poppy isn't here any more. I drove her out. She was strong. It took a while, but she crumbled in the end. They all do."

Hanna felt blood running down her arm, dripping from her fingertips on to the stone floor. Her eyes flickered involuntarily down to the dropped hockey stick at Poppy's feet.

The other girl shook her head solemnly and kicked the weapon away. "You've done enough damage with that, I think."

Poppy lurched forwards and slashed again, the tip of the scissors barely a finger's breadth from Hanna's chest.

Over Poppy's shoulder, Hanna could see Ellie lying prone by the altar, her eyes lifeless, a widening pool of blood around her head. There was no sign of Nico or Tara.

Hanna took another step backwards, desperately seeking an escape route. She made as if to dart right, on to the rows of benches, but the thing that had once been Poppy jabbed the scissors that way, herding Hanna up the aisle.

The smile on Poppy's face widened further still. Through the torn lips Hanna could see the girl's decaying gums, some sockets empty, others boasting tiny, glistering teeth that had started to poke up sharply through the torn flesh.

Hanna realized with endless horror that the other girl was changing.

When Poppy spoke, it was no longer her own voice. Instead, it was as if a dozen voices at once fell from her lips, a chorus of misery and hatred.

"I am everywhere. And I've seen you before. When I took your friend Stefan. When you led the others to the bus. When you burned my brethren last night. While they burned, I memorized your face. You angered me."

The scissors came at Hanna again. She jerked backwards and struck the rough wooden door behind her.

There was nowhere left to run.

She cried out as the blades sliced the skin just under her collarbone, the sudden splash of blood hot on her chest.

Poppy came a step closer, the rotten stench of her breath warm in Hanna's face. "I'm going to make you suffer. I'm going to kill you slowly. A little bit at a time."

In all the days since the snow had started falling, Hanna had never felt real terror. There had been times when she had known desperation, and resignation, and felt the icy touch of fear, but she had always thought that somehow she would find a way through.

Now, though, she was petrified.

Poppy's right hand came from nowhere, slapping Hanna hard across the face with her open palm. Hanna's head bounced off the door, then the sweating fingers were round her throat. Tears blurred her vision.

The creature held her there for a moment, a glimmer of triumph in the eyes that had once been Poppy's. Hanna beat at its arm frantically, pushing her feet against the wall, trying to force Poppy's face away from her own.

It was useless.

Poppy's pale skin moved closer and closer until their noses were just inches apart, the full horror of her ruined face too close for Hanna to bear.

At the edge of her vision, Hanna saw the scissors slide up into the light. They came closer and closer, the tip of the blade drifting up slowly and certainly towards Hanna's left eye.

As the light bled from the room, the last thing Hanna saw was the smile on Poppy's lips, a crimson slash splitting her pale face.

Chapter Thirty-seven

Tara had no idea why this had happened to her. It just wasn't fair.

She was always nice to people, at least to their faces, and she had so much to look forward to in life. It was as if she'd been transported into some alternative world, thrown into the middle of a terrifying horror film.

And Tara hated horror films.

While Charlie did his best to clean up the blood, dragging the bodies to the back of the church, Tara spent the hours after the attack sobbing and weeping. She wasn't sure if she was ever going to stop. Whenever the tears seemed to be drying up, she'd suddenly flash back to earlier that night, when the terrible hammering had dragged her from sleep like an electric shock.

Tara had been convinced that this was the end, and that within minutes the awful creatures would find their way inside. Then suddenly Poppy had sat up, and Tara had realized with chilling clarity that none of them had been able to see what had been happening, right under their noses.

Poppy wasn't Poppy any more.

Maybe it was the strange words Poppy had spoken or the awful noises she'd made, but Tara had shrunk into her sleeping bag and left Ellie to look on in horror. Nico had done the same, and the two of them had wriggled as far away as they could. Even so, Tara had still seen far more than she wanted.

While Hanna and Charlie had been investigating the creatures that raged outside, Poppy had attacked Ellie, smashing the side of her head against the hard stone wall again and again until all that remained was a sticky mess of blood and bone.

Just as Tara had thought it was her turn, Poppy had suddenly lurched up and gone after Hanna, slashing at her with the scissors and driving her towards the front of the chapel.

It was only when Poppy had Hanna choked against the chapel door that Tara had gone to the Austrian girl's aid. She had no idea why she'd done it, nor would she ever consider doing such a thing again. But before she'd known what was happening, she'd retrieved Hanna's lost hockey stick. And then, just as the thing that had been Poppy was about to take out one of Hanna's eyes with the scissors, she'd found herself swinging the stick with what little strength she had.

It hadn't taken Tara long to realize that her ill-advised rescue attempt had been a mistake. Poppy had barely flinched at the impact.

But somehow Tara's distraction had given Hanna enough time to snatch the scissors away from Poppy.

And Hanna had done the rest on her own.

Tara still struggled to understand what had made her rush to help Hanna, a girl she despised. Hanna antagonized and belittled her at every turn and went out of her way to make her even more miserable. But maybe it was a good thing that Tara had saved her. Maybe once Poppy had finished with Hanna, she'd have opened the door, let the other monsters in, then come back and started jabbing away with her scissors at Tara and that loser Nico.

Maybe Tara *had* done the right thing, but she still didn't feel good about it.

And even worse than the horrific attack were

the implications of Poppy's transformation. While Tara had managed to try to tell herself that Ellie had imagined seeing Malachi, changed into one of those things, wandering around in the storm, now she'd seen Poppy with her own eyes there was no denying it.

Malachi had changed.

Poppy had changed.

And that probably meant Ryan had changed, too.

Ryan wasn't coming back. Unless it was to eat Tara. Or make her like him.

Tara put her hands to her face, stared at the pool of blood by the front of the chapel, and knew that even if she did stop crying long enough to go to sleep, Poppy's hideous leer would be waiting for her, once more, in her dreams.

Chapter Thirty-eight

It was almost dawn when Charlie found Hanna.

After the attack, she'd stayed huddled up by the front door, her knees hugged to her chest, her face a watercolour mess of blood and bruise. Only the shock in her eyes had given away the fact that she was alive at all. And while Charlie had tried to clean up as many signs of the horror as he could, she'd never moved, her eyes locked on Poppy's body as it lay face down, the curved orange handle jutting out of one eye socket.

Charlie had dragged the bodies to the far side of the chapel, wiped away as much of the blood as he could, then stared up at the windows, watching the daylight struggle to gain a toehold against the darkness. Every time he'd closed his eyes, he saw a montage of images from the night before.

Ellie, sprawled on the floor, her pale eyes

unseeing, streaks of blood matting her long blond hair.

The side of her skull, caved in, the dark slick on the wall betraying the cause of the wound.

Opening his eyes with a jerk, he glanced around and realised that Hanna was gone.

She hadn't spoken since what had happened and Charlie felt sick as he searched the echoing chapel for any sign of her.

He didn't have to look far.

She was sat on the floor in the small room to the side of the altar when Charlie found her. The bottle of wine she had in her grasp was already half empty. Another one stood by her at the ready, a bottle opener next to it on the cold stone floor.

"What are you doing?"

Hanna wiped at her mouth with the back of her hand. Her breath fogged around her face when she spoke. "I'm getting drunk. I nearly died tonight. That bitch cut me to pieces. So I think I've earned this."

As if to stress her point, she took a huge swig from the bottle. Charlie stood uneasily in the doorway to the storage room, not sure what to say or do next.

Hanna looked like she had been in a car crash. There was blood down one side of her face and her left eye was crusted and blackened. She had stitched the slash on her bicep herself with the kit she had brought to treat Poppy's injuries, and a long slick of blood ran down from the clumsy needlework. The cut on her collarbone was still open and raw, a slow crimson trail seeping down her chest whenever she lifted her arm to drink.

Hanna felt Charlie's eyes studying her, and she glanced up at him warily. She sat with her back leaning against the single bed that was against the far wall. It was freezing in the small room, but Hanna didn't seem to feel it. Charlie hadn't been able to stop shaking since earlier, and as much as he tried to tell himself it was the cold he knew it wasn't.

His breath fumed in front of his eyes as he spoke. "You OK?"

Hanna put the bottle in her lap and fixed him humorously with one angry grey eye. "I'm wonderful. Why? Don't I seem it?"

She took another mammoth drag from the bottle. "I'm sorry about your friend. I liked her."

Charlie pictured Poppy, lying on the chapel

floor, the scissors protruding from her eye socket like some misshapen fungus. "I barely knew her, not before all this. But I liked her, too."

There was an uneasy silence. Hanna looked back up at Charlie, a playful smile on her torn lips. "You want to sleep with me?"

Charlie felt like he had fallen from a great height in his sleep. "What?"

"You want to sleep with me? I'm told it helps people get over times of great stress or trauma. And there's a bed just here."

Hanna tapped her bandaged hand on to the covers just behind her.

Charlie shook his head slowly. "Not right now."

Hanna laughed and took another swig from her wine. "Shame. I know I look a mess right now, but we would have enjoyed it. That girl, Leandra, had good taste. You're not bad looking."

She continued to stare at him, into him, and Charlie licked his lips warily.

"You're drunk."

Hanna's grey eye bored into him. "So?"

Charlie shook his head and sighed. "You … you want me to go?"

Hanna stared at him for a heartbeat. Then she seemed to crumble. It was as if something broke inside her, some wall that held everything at bay.

Tears shone in her eyes and she shook her head. "That thing tonight. It wasn't Poppy. It knew me. It spoke to me. It was something … else. I've never believed in anything, any greater power. But that thing…"

She wiped at her eyes then laughed bitterly. "Worst of all, the little princess saved me. How will I ever live that down?"

Hanna snorted and drained the last of the wine from her bottle. She rolled it away then started to try to open the second. Her hands shook as she fumbled with the foil on the neck of the bottle, bloodstained fingers barely managing to grip the bottle opener.

Charlie moved away from the door and sat next to her. Gently, he took the bottle away from her and put his coat around her shoulders, draping it over her like a blanket. Hanna pushed him away and shook her head.

"You don't have to do that."

Charlie ignored her and held her close so that her head rested on his shoulder. The skin of her bare arms was freezing, and her body shivered next to his.

She moaned, shook her head and sank into him. Seconds later she was fast asleep.

Chapter Thirty-nine

Hanna jerked awake on the bed in the small room by the altar. For a moment she struggled to recall where she was, what had happened, then she tried to move and her body screamed out in protest, each stabbing pain bringing with it a terrible recollection from the night before.

She rolled on to her side, saw Charlie lying next to her and tried to piece together as much as she could. The process of remembering was like walking on a beach peppered with needles and glass. There were certain places Hanna didn't want to stray too near to, jarring images that flashed up with every hesitant misstep.

Charlie stirred, saving her from a tide of grisly snapshots. Hanna stared at him with her one good eye, neither of them speaking, both struggling to process all that had happened the night before.

It was Charlie that buckled first. Hanna watched

him struggle up, heard his footsteps take him out towards the back of the chapel. Freezing air caressed her skin from the blast of wind as he unchained the door. When Charlie came back into the room, he held a small bowl in his hand, filled with snow and ice.

Hanna's voice sounded far away in the cotton wool of her head. "Anything?"

Charlie shook his head. "It's still snowing. Still stormy. But I'm pretty sure those things went as soon as you killed Poppy."

Hanna felt herself start to tremble at the memory, and she struggled up to a sitting position, catching sight of herself in the mirror over the sink.

The creature looking back at her resembled a walking corpse. Much of her skin was coated in dried blood, most of it her own, and her face was bruised and swollen. Her left eye was almost sealed shut. She glanced down at her chest and arm, catching glimpses of the cuts there, unsure as to how bad things were going to get.

Charlie took a cloth and some antiseptic from the medical bag by the bed and dipped the cloth in the wet snow. Hanna watched him and took a deep breath when he started to clean and wash her cuts.

"How are you feeling?"

Hanna felt her one good eye flick open and closed. "My head's pounding. I hurt all over. But I'll live."

Charlie dabbed the blood from her neck and she tasted the sour, dry alcohol lingering on her tongue when she spoke. "Thank you."

Charlie shrugged. "You don't need to thank me. I'd have died a long time ago without you."

She groaned while he cleaned a split on her top lip then peered at him through one slitted eye. "I don't think so."

Hanna drew in a sharp intake of breath, her mind flicking through the past few days. She heard the words tumble out before she could stop them, felt tears hot and unwelcome on her cheeks. "I was going to use you. All of you. To find out what those things were. If they had anything to do with what happened to my brother. They never found his body, you know. I always knew that wasn't right. I was going to use you all to find out what I could. I was going to do whatever it took."

Charlie shook his head and gently cleaned the wound on Hanna's collarbone. "But you didn't."

Hanna hissed as the cotton caught the edge of the cut, tugging at the skin. "The others?"

Charlie looked away and shook his head slowly from side to side. "Ellie's dead. She came with me, the night when the hostel burned down, to look for you. She was braver than the rest. Kinder. It seems so unfair. And Poppy... Well, you know what happened to her."

Hanna nodded slowly. "And the other one. The one with the orange hat?"

Charlie washed the cloth in the bowl, turning the snow pink. "Tara and him, they both hid when it started. Poppy sat up, grabbed Ellie, smashed in her skull. Nico said he hid under the sleeping bags, closed his eyes and waited for it to be over."

She pictured Nico, buried under a sea of quilts, praying that some divine force would transport him elsewhere, while Poppy dissected Hanna one cut at a time. "He froze. Useful."

Charlie shook his head. "You can't blame him."

Despite herself, Hanna felt a flicker of a smile tug at her torn lips. "I'd rather it had been him that saved me than the little princess."

"I'm glad somebody did."

Their eyes met again and Hanna found herself forced to look away, overcome by the rush of emotions that swept over her. Charlie blushed, then dabbed at the stitches on Hanna's arm, gently cleaning around the pale, puckered skin. It was freezing inside the small room, and goosebumps rose on Hanna's pale flesh. She grunted as the cloth tugged at a rogue stitch, and then sighed and rubbed at her head.

"So when you found me last night … what happened? My head's pounding, not just from being slapped, and the taste in my mouth…"

"You were drunk. I put you to bed. That was all."

Hanna closed her good eye and tried to piece together what she had said to him. "You're a good liar. Where are the others now?"

Charlie glanced back over his shoulder. "Asleep."

They stared at each other for a moment, both aware that there was something neither of them dared to mention. In the end, Charlie asked the question, even though Hanna was fairly sure he must have known the answer himself.

"What the hell happened to Poppy?"

Hanna drew the blanket around her shoulders.

"It … it terrifies me to think of it. It was like she was possessed. She wasn't herself. Her voice. The noises that came out of her. The things she said. The way that those things outside just stopped when she caught hold of me. And her strength. I think she was changing, Charlie. Changing into one of *them*. I don't know why I didn't realize it sooner. And if Tara hadn't had come over when she did…"

Hanna stopped before the tears could come and reached out with a shaking hand, catching the front of Charlie's jumper. "I can't do this on my own. I thought I could. But I can't."

In the pale dawn light, Charlie looked suddenly older, the beginnings of stubble on his chin, his hair jutting out at unnatural angles, a scarring knowledge in his eyes from all the things he'd seen.

He squeezed Hanna's fingers. "You don't have to. Whatever we do, whatever happens, we're in this together. I promise."

Chapter Forty

Nico sat behind the altar, his sleeping bag pulled up to his chin, his eyes fixed on Charlie as he made his way to the heavy wooden door at the front of the chapel. Next to him Tara slept, but from the way she moaned and thrashed, her dreams were anything but peaceful.

The open space of the church echoed as Charlie undid the heavy metal latch, pulled the door open a fraction, then closed it behind him. The keening wail of the wind rose for a moment then was quickly cut off. Nico lay back in the nest of coats and blankets he'd made for himself, trying his best not to think about all that had happened hours before.

After a while, the heavy door swung open again. Charlie came back into the chapel and made his way down the aisle and past the pews. His dark hair hung into his eyes, and his khaki jacket was covered in snowflakes, the laces on his boots leaving a trail of snow as he walked.

Nico heard his own voice bounce off the cold walls as Charlie came closer. "What's it like out there?"

Charlie seemed to come out of a daze and he made his way towards Nico and sat down in front of him. "Cold. It's more exposed up here, I suppose, and that wind bites right through you."

"I'm guessing it's still snowing."

Charlie nodded. "As much as ever. What time is it?"

Nico looked down at his Lego Batman watch, a gift from his mother. He pictured her for a moment, thousands of miles away in Bristol, going insane with stress and worry. When he spoke, his voice trembled and shook. "Seven fifty-five. Feels later. It's like I don't even need to sleep any more. It's like I can't stay asleep now after all the things I've seen."

Nico watched as Charlie's eyes drifted towards the bloody smear on the rough stone across from them. Charlie had tried to wash away the hair and bone but the blood was harder to shift. Nico felt a twist of nausea in his stomach and nodded towards the front door. "Those things, are they…?"

Charlie shook his head. "No. There's nothing. Even their footprints are nearly gone. The walls are scratched, there's nail marks on the wood. But I think it'll hold another night. It's weird, but it seems like … like they didn't really want to get in at all."

Nico stared at the far door. "I might be useless in a fight, but I do know my vampire lore. And in most of the films I've seen, vampires aren't allowed on holy ground. Maybe they just couldn't come in."

There was a noise from their right and Hanna stepped gingerly into the room. She had her blue ski jacket on, her beanie pulled down low on her head. Strands of black hair poked out from under the hat, obscuring her swollen eye and much of her face. She glanced down at Nico and sighed.

"Well, that's a reason to think everything's going to be all right, then, isn't it?"

For a moment Nico studied Hanna's face. She looked like she had done three minutes in a cage-fighting arena. After a few seconds he found his words again.

"The stories must come from somewhere. If that old man said they'd been around for ages, then surely they must have fed into the myths and stories we hear? Vampires don't come out in the day. These things don't. And they can't go into churches. So maybe these can't."

Hanna stared at him for a moment then shook her head. "We don't know what these things are. And I'm not going to risk my life on something that you've picked up from *Dungeons and Dragons*, or from some episode of *Buffy the Vampire Slayer*. We need to be realistic. There are only four of us left now. We might not last another night."

She let her words hang in the frosty air for a moment, then spoke again. "No help is going to come, not with the weather like this. We're going to starve, freeze or those things are going to find a way in. And after what happened to Poppy, I think we all know what might happen then."

Next to Nico, Tara had stirred and she yawned loudly. She stared up at Hanna with bleary eyes and shook her head. "Thanks for waking me up with such a bright, happy prediction. I don't know what we'd do without you. It's been four days now since anyone contacted home, since anyone's heard from us. This will be the fifth. And we should have been on the way home by now. My mother will be having a shitfit. In fact, she's probably over here, in Austria, right now, raising hell. Someone will come and find us."

Hanna shook her head wearily. "And what can she do? Make the weather stop? Threaten those things out there with her Gucci handbag? Perhaps Mummy can jump on her broomstick and fly up here? You don't get it, do you? They're not going to let us go. They know we're here. They won't lift the storm until they've found us. And nobody can get a helicopter up here. Nobody can climb or drive and the lift is fragged. That's why it's cheap to get here and stay here, because it's in the middle of nowhere, with one way in and one way out. We're not in Zell am See, Mayrhofen or St Anton! We're not getting rescued! Get that into your stupid empty head!"

Hanna was breathing hard after her rant and she reached out a hand on to the altar to support herself. "Think about what Poppy said. *The caves where the rocks are kissed by diamonds.* I know where that is. Poppy said that there were some of your friends there. That maybe they were alive."

Tara shrugged. "Poppy wasn't Poppy any more. She was going to kill us all."

Hanna shook her head. "I'm going to go up there. I'm going to put an end to all of this."

Her words sent a current of fear through Nico, and he stared at her, aghast, before he finally managed to splutter out a weak denial. "What, just walk up there and knock on the door of these caves? You must be out of your mind. There could be hundreds of those things there."

Hanna smiled grimly. "I hope so. But even if there aren't, what if there *are* people there? What if they've changed into those things? What if Ryan's there, or Stefan? What if my *brother's* there? You're going to just leave them like that?"

Tara shrugged. "There's nobody that I like enough to make me go out there and go looking for those things. Not even Ryan."

Nico took a deep breath. He was terrified, but at the same time there was no way he wanted to stay on his own in the chapel.

Tara shook her head defiantly. "I'm not going. There's no way."

There was a long pause before Hanna broke the silence. "You can stay here and wait to die if you want. Wait for those things to find a way in. Wait

311

for them to do to you what they've done to everyone else. But I'm not going to."

Hanna turned towards Charlie questioningly. He looked her up and down and smiled gently. "You can barely stand."

Hanna shrugged. "All the more reason to go now, before I fall over. I've just swallowed a load of painkillers. You don't need to worry about me."

Charlie sighed. "This place, these caves. How far away are they?"

Hanna glanced up at the stained-glass windows in the ceiling, as if she was measuring the daylight. "They're walkable. Especially now we don't have Poppy slowing us down. They're not far from here and there's a lift station, a big one, on the way, with supplies. Things we can use. If we go now, we can be at the caves before dark."

Nico pondered her words, wondering exactly what might be in the lift station that would be of use for Hanna's suicide mission. Over by the lectern, Charlie's eyes were thoughtful. "Say we get there. Say we get to these caves and they are full of those things. Or there are some of the other students from our school, still alive. Or …

like Poppy. What do we do then?"

Hanna rubbed gently at her bruised eye, and swore quietly in German. "I have a plan. That's why we're stopping at the lift station. At the very least, we won't have to sit and wait for them to tear us to pieces."

Tara rolled her eyes in disbelief. "The last time you had a plan you burned down the hostel we were hiding in and nearly killed us all."

Hanna glared at her icily, and Nico braced himself for her eruption.

"Let me think, was that the time that it was probably your bitching and whining that gave us away? The time those things would have surely torn you to pieces if I hadn't incinerated dozens of them before they could get to you? Is that the plan you mean? The plan that saved your life?"

Tara shrugged, beaten, and Hanna pressed on.

"You sit here if you want to, sit here and freeze and starve and wait to die. Maybe you'll get lucky and whoever finds you one day might find you frozen solid rather than turned into one of those things. But I'm not going to sit here and wait."

Hanna was angry now, tears of rage glistening

in her one good eye. She turned to face Charlie and chewed at her scabbed lip. "What about you? You spoke to that old man with me. He knew what was going on, he was part of it, he could have done something about what happens here. If we don't try to find those things, try to put a stop to this, we're just as bad as he was. If we die here, then five years from now, ten, it will happen again. And what if there are some of your friends up there, changing? You want to make it up to your father, like you said you did, then there's no better time than now."

Nico reckoned that Charlie bristled at Hanna's words, but he swallowed down any angry reply. "They're not my friends. Nobody even spoke to me before a week ago. But I'll come with you. I don't have any better ideas."

Hanna glanced around at the three of them that were left. "Well, I do. And if they're down there, if they're in those caves, I'm going to pay them back for everything they've taken from me."

Chapter Forty-one

Hanna felt Charlie's eyes on her as she filled her tatty rucksack with the small, cylindrical yellow-and-red tubes. They had an almost comical appearance and a strange, sweet odour, reminiscent of confectionary.

Hanna paused in her actions and glanced up at him. She noticed that her hands were shaking slightly, traces of blood under her nails, an unwelcome reminder of the night before.

Charlie pointed down at the red tube that poked out of the bag. "You're sure they're safe?"

Hanna nodded slowly. "Perfectly. Until you take the cap off. And then…"

Hanna didn't need to finish the sentence.

She had dragged them across the mountain, to the lift station she knew waited there. It had been locked, bolted, but Hanna had used her hockey stick to smash the glass, fished through a series of keys to the containers inside, and found the explosives she was looking for. She tried to mask how fragile she felt, but she wasn't sure she was convincing anyone, least of all herself. Before they'd left the chapel, Hanna had dug a pack of painkillers out of the first-aid kit and taken as many as she dared. She wanted to numb the pain, but at the same time she needed to think straight.

"We need to get moving. It's not far now, but we need to be there before dark."

She transferred the last of the tubes of dynamite to the rucksack then passed it to Charlie. He took it off her nervously, and peered inside. "So how does this stuff work?"

Hanna shrugged. "With this, you don't even need a match. Pull off the end, it lights automatically. And down goes the snow."

Charlie eyed her warily. "You used these before?"

Hanna thought back to a life gone by. "Once or twice. I've been on ski patrol a few times, across the valley, last year when the snow was really heavy. We went up in helicopters, picked out the slopes that were most dangerous, and set them off. The patrol, they fly over, drop these. There's no mystery to it."

"And you think it will work?"

"Those things burn. So I think it's safe to assume dynamite will work, too. And if not, if they are in those caves, we can bury them so deep they'll never come out again."

Charlie nodded, then reached down onto the floor next to one of the containers. There was something else there, a red plastic pistol, more like a child's toy than anything of use. Hanna had dismissed it, but Charlie picked up the flare gun, checked that it was loaded and placed it carefully into the rucksack.

Hanna was about to ask him if he knew how to use it when she was interrupted by Nico's voice by the door. Behind him, the redundant lifts rocked back and forth in the gale outside, a mournful reminder of the world far below.

Nico stood next to Tara, a CB radio clutched hopefully in one hand. Hanna shook her head dismissively.

"Don't bother. There's no way the signal from that would cut through this storm. You might as well attach a note to a rock and throw that down into the valley."

Nico ignored her and flicked up the switch on

the central unit, a faded red light blinking into life to signify the presence of power. A low static buzz rose from the radio. Despite herself, Hanna felt her heartbeat quicken. Tara sighed and walked across to sit in the station's single chair, spinning once then placing her feet on the wooden floor. Hanna had heard Charlie talking to Tara as they ploughed through the storm, and Tara had made it clear that her desire to not be on her own only just outweighed her reluctance to accompany them.

Nico lifted the receiver to his mouth, clicked on the button by his thumb, and started to speak. "If you're out there … if you're listening … please. Is anyone out there? Can you hear this?"

Hanna swore quietly and shook her head. Tara leaned forwards in her chair, her eyes locked on the radio unit. They waited expectantly, their hopes slowly eroded by the dead static. Nico stared at the receiver imploringly then spoke into it again, louder this time. "Is anyone there? Does anyone know what's happening up here? They trapped us here with the storm. The teachers, the adults, they were gone, just … gone. And when the blizzard got so bad that we could barely open the door, those things came out. And they've been hunting us ever since. Please. There are only four of us now. They took the rest. And we're not going to last another night. It's going to be dark soon and they'll come out again. If you can hear this, if you're out there, please..."

The wind rocked the wooden building, the derelict lifts above them squeaking painfully on their wires in a vain attempt to break free. But the radio stayed silent. Hanna shook her head, walked over to Nico and gently took the receiver from his hand.

"We're on our own. And if we don't go soon, we'll be gone, too. We need to move."

Tara took a step away from the others, as if drawing an imaginary line to separate them. "I'm not doing this. I don't want to do this. And you can't make me."

Hanna pointed away into the distance. "Those rocks over there, the cliffs. That's where we're going. It's not far now."

Tara stamped her foot on the wooden floor. "No. No way. No more. Ryan's gone. They've all gone. And I'm not going any further."

Hanna stared at Tara, the mixture of terror and fury on her face convincing Hanna that there was

319

little point arguing. "You can wait, then. You can shelter here."

She glanced at Charlie. "All of you can, if that's what you want. But I'm going in. I haven't come all this way to freeze and rot here."

Nico rummaged about in his pocket and brought out a black plastic torch. He clicked it on and off then shook his head. "I can't, I don't think. Caves. Darkness. I know we should, but I don't want to leave Tara on her own. And I wouldn't be any use, anyway."

Tara nodded gratefully, took a step closer to Nico, then glared at Hanna.

"I only left the church with you because I didn't want to be on my own. Not because I'm going to help you. And the doors weren't going to hold another night, not if those things came back."

She touched the bare skin around her neck and ran shaking fingers through her hair. "And my cross. I know it sounds stupid, but I lost my cross last night, the silver one that Ryan gave me. So I'm staying. That's it."

Tears started to brim in her eyes, and she turned towards Nico. "We're staying, right?"

Nico nodded slowly – glad, Hanna thought, of the last-minute reprieve offered to him, and forgetful of all the times Tara had insulted him. Hanna licked her frayed lips and stared at Charlie. The question was there, even though she didn't speak.

Charlie reached out and took Hanna's hand in his.

"I'm with you," Charlie whispered. "I'm with you till the end."

Chapter Forty-two

By the time they saw the entrance to the caves, the sky was darkening, the faint patch of light in the heavens fading away, as if the sun had never really risen at all behind the thick layer of cloud.

It hadn't taken them long to reach the rock-face, their pace quickening as if in a desire to bring things to an end one way or another. They had staggered doggedly up across a deserted piste, pines on one side, a jagged rock-face on the other, a mountain peak high above them.

Even though she walked him right past the gap that led though the rocks, Charlie would have missed the hidden entrance if Hanna hadn't paused and raised her glove to signal for him to stop. Charlie staggered to a halt, glanced to his left and saw the space in the rock-face, an entrance peppered with shining shards of rock like precious stones. As Hanna had said, no one but a local would know of the caves.

He gazed at Hanna questioningly. "Here?"

She nodded, and lowered her scarf. "This has to be where Poppy meant. It's not far now, just through here."

Hanna ducked down, vanishing through the gap, and Charlie wiped at his leaking nose before following her. The entrance widened into a short, straight passageway then into daylight a few seconds later. Charlie blinked at the bright light then caught up with Hanna, who was waiting in a snow-covered field, a frozen, craggy wall of grey rock behind her. A long powder trail led away, between two-rock faces, the blizzard hiding where its path lay.

"Sometimes, when I was little, my brother would bring a few of us over this way, into this part of the mountains. Nobody was supposed to come here. The old folk in the village said these paths were cursed, haunted, but that just made us all the more keen to come and ski through here. But I never thought..."

She shook her head, turned and stared at the wall of rock in the distance, then pointed to a jagged slash in the stone, just visible through the falling snow. "That's where we're going. The caves are just through there."

Charlie stared at the opening and felt a deep, hollow fear gnaw away in the pit of his stomach, a desire to turn and run back to where they had left the others. "Did you ever explore them? Did your brother take you in when you were little?"

Hanna scratched at the bandage on her hand. "No. There was a landslide further down the mountain, and the caves here were always said to be very unstable, the rocks not steady. This was one place we didn't ever go near."

"Do you think they knew? Your parents? About those things?"

Hanna shook her head with certainty. "They lived here for a while, but they came from the north originally, near Salzburg, a long way from here. I think they suspected, perhaps, that this place wasn't … right somehow. They never felt accepted here. The people in the mountains, they always kept themselves to themselves, they don't pry, they don't ask. I don't think my parents ever really felt at home here, like they belonged, but for me, when I came back, it was perfect, for a while. Just me, the mountains and my memories of Jon."

Hanna's eyes misted up as she spoke her brother's name and Charlie took her hand in his. There was no going back now.

They trudged the short distance through the waist-deep snow towards the entrance to the cave. The inky blackness inside was so complete that Charlie once again had to fight the urge to turn and run. Instead he looked up at the grey sky above their heads and pulled a torch out of his coat pocket, checking it one last time. Hanna watched him, a sad smile tugging at her lips.

"Last chance to turn back."

Charlie bit his bottom lip. "I don't have anything better to do right now. There are a million places I'd rather be. But there's no one I'd rather be with."

Hanna looked down at the snow. "A few days ago, when we sat in that bar together, I realized we were the same, you and me. And I suppose it's because … I saw something in you, when we first met on the mountain. Something that reminded me of myself. A part of me that didn't care any more. A part of me that was just sick of it all."

Hanna reached out and took his hand. "I'm

sorry for what I said this morning, the way I spoke to you. Your father would be so proud of you, you know. You put others before yourself, through all of this, that's what you've done."

Charlie glanced across at her. "And you haven't?"

Hanna shook her head slowly. "No, not really. All I wanted was revenge. That's why I stayed. I'd have done anything to get it. It's almost the only thing that's keeping me standing now."

"Almost?"

Hanna stared at him for a moment, her one grey eye unreadable, then she reached out, grabbed the front of his coat and pulled him to her. Her lips were cold and rough, the fingers that brushed his cheek like shards of ice, but all the same Charlie didn't want the moment to end. He kissed her back, and then Hanna pulled away and shook her head.

"I'm sorry," she mumbled, "but I didn't want to miss the chance to do that."

Charlie smiled. "Neither did I."

He shook his head. When he spoke, his heartbeat was a jagged lump in his throat. "Shit, I'm scared. If we don't go now…"

Hanna nodded and took his hand in hers, and they slipped into the darkness.

Chapter Forty-three

Charlie followed Hanna into the dark, stealing one last glimpse of the daylight before he entered the cave. They had both taken heavy lanterns from the ski-patrol hut. Ice on the rough, pocked walls reflected the dull electric light, the faintest noises amplified as they trod deeper into the gloom, the howl of the storm, faint droplets of water in the distance. The cave widened, so that it stretched high above their heads, the dancing lights casting frenetic, indiscernible shadows everywhere they looked.

The passage ahead was partially blocked by rockfall, and they scrambled over the rubble. Charlie was slower, trying not to catch his lantern on the debris. Hanna waited for him, then they continued further into the passageway.

They hadn't gone more than a few metres before Hanna paused and whispered for Charlie to stop, her attention locked on a dark patch smeared on the uneven wall of the tunnel. There were four long dark marks there, as if a hand had dragged at the rock, trying to gain purchase with bloody fingers before being taken further underground. Hanna held her lantern up close to the wall, then took a deep breath, glanced at Charlie, and carried on into the darkness.

Ahead of them the cavern widened again. Charlie pulled his backpack off his shoulder, checked that its contents were still there, ready to grab if need be.

Charlie found his back wet with sweat, sweltering in his heavy coat and beanie, his heart pounding like a drum in his chest as the cave narrowed slightly. Hanna paused, glancing down at the floor where an item of discarded clothing lay.

A dirty cardigan, old and torn. There were dark splashes on the wool, but Charlie didn't hesitate to investigate them further. A few more echoing steps, and a tiny sock lay in the glow of their lanterns, green cartoon snakes embroidered into the material, something that might have been worn by a child not yet in school.

Hanna's pace quickened and she pressed on, leading Charlie into another opening, wider this time. She stopped suddenly, and Charlie drew up alongside her and shone his lantern into the hollow beyond.

In the centre of the cave was what looked like a huge pile of rags, a mountain of them, so high that it reached almost to the jagged ceiling above. Charlie took a step closer and realized that among the pile were coats, jumpers, trousers, shirts, all of it thrown together in a vast, ragged mound. Some of them looked less aged, the styles more modern, and Charlie recognized several logos that he knew emblazoned on the discarded clothes. Other items among the pile were ripped and torn and faded as if they had lain there lost for centuries.

Over to the left was a natural alcove in the rock, and a shining pile rested on the floor there. Hanna walked over to the glow, as if in a trance, reached down and picked up a long, thin piece of twine, a tiny golden talisman at the end dancing in the shadows. Charlie crept closer to see that the pile was a treasure trove of jewellery, rings, chains, pendants and charms, the gold and silver glistening like ice in the twilight.

He shook his head. "We should go. We need

to go. This place… It's terrible. Let's just light the dynamite, set it off, run. While we still can."

Hanna was silent. She looked at Charlie, and he saw that tears were welling in her eyes. "This was my brother's. This was Jon's. It *was* them, after all. It was those things that took him."

Charlie peered closer at the twine, and saw a tiny dolphin at the end of the material. Hanna wrapped it around her bandaged knuckles and looked back up at Charlie.

"You go if you have to, but I can't. They brought Jon here. He might still be here, now. I need to know. I need to know the truth. And I need to finish this."

Chapter Forty-four

Hanna's body was a shimmering mass of pain, the vision in her right eye reduced to a thin strip of light. Her head pounded, and the cuts on her bicep and across her collarbone leaked fresh blood through her shirt whenever she moved.

Every step made her hurt. But anger kept her going.

She sensed, rather than saw, Charlie's presence just behind her, the gentle crunch of his feet, his deep, uneasy breathing.

He had been right. The place, the caves, were terrible, like something out of the worst nightmare imaginable. But even if Charlie had refused to go with her, she would still have gone on alone into the darkness.

Hanna squeezed her fist and felt the small dolphin talisman bite into her skin. Jon had worn it everywhere he went, his lucky charm. It had been given to him by their granddad, long dead now, a souvenir from days in the Navy. Jon had said once that he thought it kept him safe, gifted him good fortune when things turned bad.

In the end, Hanna supposed, it had done Jon no good at all. But even so, it gave her a strange confidence, as if her brother watched over her.

She knew Charlie was scared, and that if she had agreed, he would have fled back to the daylight in a heartbeat, but her fear was gone now, the terror from the night before, all of it fused into a cold, burning fury. She squeezed the charm in her fist tighter still, felt it pierce the skin on her palm, one more in an intricate map of dozens of cuts and wounds and slashes. She would do this for Jon, this one last thing.

And then perhaps she would see him again.

Hanna paused for a second, unzipped the pocket of the backpack and shone her lantern on to its contents. She had shared the dynamite between their two rucksacks, and she spotted the red plastic of the flare gun poking out from between the sticks, its thick, clumsy crimson barrel like something from a cartoon. She glanced back at Charlie, nodded at him and stumbled a few steps further, into an area where the caverns widened once more.

And then she froze.

The electric glow of the lanterns revealed a large, round cavern, wider than all the rest they had seen, the walls pitted with dozens of alcoves, places where the rock had eroded away over time. In each of the alcoves, by the glare of the lantern, Hanna could see sleeping figures, their eyes closed, their awful jaws sealed shut, the tatty rags of clothing that covered them shifting faintly with their breathing. It was like a painting, she thought, an awful rendering of an image from some medieval world of horror.

And then Hanna heard a voice, familiar and at the same time foreign, and she turned to see the worst sight of all.

In the centre of the room was a throne, a pile of clothes and rags and old newspapers with a roughly hewn wooden chair atop it, which in time had been encircled and enwrapped and overgrown by the debris around it. Among the paper and clothing and detritus, Hanna could just make out the bulbous edges of skulls and bones, and other shapes that she had no desire to linger on for too long.

A thin woman sat in the chair, her dark eyes fixed

on Hanna, the hint of a smile on her red lips, a faded white dress hanging from her gaunt shoulders. She could have been beautiful, with her long dark hair and pale skin, but as her smile widened and Hanna saw her small, sharp teeth, she felt a cold chill at the back of her skull. Charlie stepped alongside Hanna, swore and placed his lantern on the ground, his eyes wide.

The woman's mouth opened wider, splitting her face like a shark's, and her words filled the chamber, the sound a mixture of the voices of dozens of souls, intertwined, speaking all as one.

"Welcome. Welcome to our home. My name is Sabine."

Hanna realized where she had seen that cold smile before, her mind flashing back to the night before when Poppy had slashed and hacked at her with the scissors.

Sabine's voice was rich with dust and decay, a trickle of mirth running through her words.

"I thought this might finish last night. That I could use Poppy to drag you outside to my children. You were wise to rest in the church. It's one place they won't tread. Poppy wouldn't have stood it for long, once she fully became one of us. But it doesn't matter. Poppy did what I needed her to do. I knew if she told you where we were, if she whispered the way, you'd come to me. You've caused me so much trouble these past few days, cost me so many of my children. Without you, without you two, the others would have been dead in hours."

The woman took a deep breath and glanced down to Hanna's bandaged hand, and the golden talisman that hung from the crusted blood.

"So you found my treasury. You like that one? You can keep it, for the little time you have left."

Hanna found herself fighting the urge to scream, to shout her hatred, to run at the creature on the throne and gouge at her eyes, tear her to pieces. Instead, she took a deep breath and nodded slowly. "It belonged to someone I loved very much. My brother."

The light in the woman's eyes flickered for a moment and she stared at Hanna with fresh curiosity. When she spoke again there was something else in her eyes, a wariness that hadn't been there before.

"I remember him. I remember them all. Some fill our bellies. Others I make into my children. Jon, wasn't it? He fought us. He was too strong to join us. But we used him all the same and his meat helped us to sleep these last few years. Is that why you've fought so hard, for so long? For him?"

The woman's question hung in the air, the eerie echo of dozens of voices ringing in Hanna's ears. Gently, a millimetre at a time, Hanna started to bring up the rucksack and its deadly contents.

Charlie swore softly next to her, and out of the corner of her good eye she noticed him staring at the alcoves, mesmerized by the sight of the twisted figures that were starting to stir and twitch. Some of them, Hanna realized, had arrived in the same school party as Charlie, several of the pupils, one of their teachers, their faces different now, their eyes slowly flickering open. Malachi, who had vanished into the storm days ago with Ryan, sat sleeping in one of the alcoves, his fingers curled into talons, his once handsome face now bulbous and malformed.

Sabine ran her pale white fingers along the arms of her chair then glanced up at the two of them. "I can't let you leave here. You've led us a merry dance, but no more. Once it's dark, my children will find your friends. And then we'll sleep again."

Hanna studied the folds of dry, aged paper at the bottom of the makeshift throne, and she brought the bag a fraction higher. "What are you? Vampires?"

Sabine chuckled, her eyes raking the walls of the cave.

"So much more. These are my children. They are chained to me, beholden to me, unable to stray too far from their mother, to venture too far from my side. But my power runs through them. My whispers tell them what to do. My blood runs in their veins. I have been here since the start, cursed to live out eternity in these mountains. Our numbers have diminished, but all the same, here I rule."

Hanna shook her head slowly, her fingers another inch closer. "They know, don't they, the villagers? And they never tell?"

The woman nodded slowly, the smile widening with delight. Hanna moved her fingers again, felt the plastic brush her fingertips.

"Why did you … why did you take the adults, the teachers that brought the students to Kaldgellan?"

Sabine glanced towards the side of the cavern, to a black-haired, olive-skinned girl, her eyes flickering open just inside the hood of her bloodstained top. Her checked trainers, Hanna noticed, were sprayed with crimson.

"Kelsey," Charlie whispered, and Hanna moved again, felt the butt of the flare gun slip into her palm. The woman stared at Charlie for a heartbeat then met Hanna's eyes. For a moment she was back in the chapel hours before, Poppy leaning over her with the scissors in her hand.

She felt goosebumps prickle her skin.

"Fear makes the hunt so much sweeter and the feeding so much more satisfying. And the young are so much richer. We wanted to drain every last drop that we could from you. Enough so we could dream for winter upon winter, our bellies full, our minds far away."

Hanna started to lift the gun out of the bag into the light, slowly, so slowly. The smile on Sabine's face fell away, as if at the flick of a switch, and her voice boomed in the depths of the cave. All around them, on the walls, dozens of sets of eyes flashed wide open, focusing balefully on the two figures in the centre of the cave.

"You think you can hurt me before my creatures

fall upon you? Before they tear you limb from limb?"

Hanna met the woman's dark eyes and held the gun tightly in her throbbing palm, the weapon still hidden just inside the bag. She shook her head bitterly. "You think I care? I'm ready to die. And you killed my brother, you bitch."

Sabine's hands curled into claws, sharp, dirty nails digging into the arms of her wooden throne. She leaned forwards, her words low and venomous.

"I'll make your death slow. You're too pure to turn, so I'll let my children eat you, piece by piece, while you watch. First your friend, then you. I'll make your pain last for hours. Days. The villagers will whisper your name and know the terror and dread that awaits them if they ever speak of us."

All around the cave, the figures started to unfurl their limbs from the alcoves, slowly, hypnotically, like spiders descending from a web. Hanna gritted her teeth and got ready to try to pull the trigger before the creatures could reach her.

And then the screaming started.

Tara's voice, somewhere behind them, long and high, echoed off the walls of the cave, drowning out every other sound. For a moment, just for a heartbeat, Sabine's eyes flicked to the mouth of the cave, to the two figures that had just emerged into the cavern. That moment was all Hanna needed. She raised the gun, pulled the trigger.

An instant later the whole world seemed to turn into an inferno.

The flare from Hanna's gun struck the newspaper at the foot of the tattered throne, the clothing and rags around it catching fire instantly. The flames reached up into the air in a heartbeat, around the chair, engulfing the pale-skinned woman, catching in her hair, peeling away her skin. Her screams joined those of Tara, and all around the cavern the creatures writhed and screamed in horrifying unison.

Hanna felt a hand pull at her arm, and she turned away from the blazing throne and saw Charlie's face, inches from her own. "Go! Move!"

He pulled Hanna to the mouth of the cave, just as a skeletal, blackened figure slipped from atop the pyre at the centre of the cave and tumbled down on to the floor. Dark eyes burned in the red running wax that had been Sabine's face, framed by smouldering strands of black hair. She glared at Hanna, and her charred lips moved feverishly.

"Kill them! Kill them all!"

Charlie pushed Hanna in the back, hard, sending her flying towards the entrance to the cave. Nico was there, a look of pure terror on his face, Tara next to him, her mouth open, ready to scream once more.

Then Charlie's fingers were wrapped in Hanna's and they were scrambling down the corridor, heat at their back, screams in their ears, a terrible stench of burning flesh in their nostrils. Their lanterns were forgotten but the blaze from behind them lit the way.

They burst out of the tunnel and Hanna felt something land on her back, a heavy, twitching shape, and her legs gave out, the stones rushing up to meet her. From the floor of the cave, she could see dozens of creatures sprinting towards them, struggling to get out of the tunnel. Some were on fire, their ragged clothing in turn lighting those nearest to them. Their faces were twisted in jagged masks of hatred, their skin red and seared. But still it didn't stop them.

Charlie had hold of the flare gun and he

smashed the butt of the weapon into the face of the creature that had fallen on Hanna's back, knocking it into two other shapes that sprawled blindly from the cave beyond. Off to Hanna's left, Tara was screaming, a bulky figure pulling at her arm as if she was a doll, trying to dig its serrated teeth into the exposed skin on her wrist.

As stars danced in front of her eyes, Hanna realized with immense horror that the creature Tara wrestled with had once been Ryan.

Hanna watched Nico hit at the creature with the stick he held in his gloved hand, saw it reel away. Then she turned and dug into the rucksack, pulled out the first stick of dynamite she came to, and unscrewed the cap, her mind a blank. She felt the fuse light, and watched the charge start to burn down, wondering what she would feel first, the heat of the flames, or the teeth ripping into her flesh.

Before either could happen, a hand reached down, clutched the lit dynamite and lifted it away. Hanna glanced up, saw the blood on Nico's neck, the numb look in his eyes. He turned and ran at the creatures that were stumbling closer, the dynamite still clutched in his hand, and the smouldering figures fell upon him like wolves. Hanna scrambled to her feet and saw Charlie rushing to Nico's aid. She grabbed his coat, pulling him back with the little strength she had left.

The words fell out of her mouth in a mad scramble. "You can't help him! You can't! He's been bitten! It's going to blow, all of it! *Scheisse*, move! Go!"

Charlie's expression turned from bewilderment to realisation, and he grabbed Hanna, and started to run. Hanna left the rucksack with the rest of the dynamite abandoned on the cave floor and ran for her life. Tara was just ahead of them, on the way out of the caves. The flames from behind them still showed the way, but now the faintest pale glimmer showed in front of them, lighting the way to salvation beyond.

Suddenly the world began to rumble, a series of explosions that seemed to shake Hanna's world to its foundations. The cave, the floor, everything slid sideways, righted itself then tumbled away once more. Fresh, cool air bit into her lungs, and she fell, felt Charlie dragging her desperately into the light.

Another rumble, much bigger than before, like thunder dead overhead, and Hanna's ears seemed to scream with the force of it. Her eyes were closed, all fight gone from her, and as she felt Charlie's fingers slip away from hers, she sensed something falling over them, embracing them, like a vast, heavy quilt. And then she knew no more.

Chapter Forty-five

Charlie was stuck in a dream. He was underground, in caves full of dark water, swimming, drowning, twisting, turning. Nightmarish faces of people he had known washed around him, wide mouths open in a rictus of pain and hatred. Something was on his back, pressing him down, crushing the breath out of him with its weight, suffocating him.

But then fingers brushed his own, enwrapping his hand, starting to pull him in a different direction. He glanced up from the gloomy depths, saw a face he recognized, that of his father. He felt the fingers drag him up towards the light.

Then he opened his eyes.

He was face down in a huge pile of snow and rock, debris all around him, the rough upturned earth and ice tumbling away as he struggled to his feet. At first he had no idea where he was, then it all came back to him and he spun round, expecting to see a horde of burning pursuers rushing at him.

But where once there had been the forbidding entrance to the caves beyond, now there was only a huge, broken wall of rock. Snow had fallen from above, huge waves of it, and it had swept Charlie away from the tunnels, washed him further down the slope.

He spat into the snow, looked down at his fingers and realized that he was no longer holding Hanna's hand.

Panic filled his world and he scrambled about madly, searching, digging. Something caught his eye, metres away, a flash of colour amidst the monotone, and he staggered over and grabbed the back of a coat, pulling it and its owner up to the surface. Tara's eyes fluttered open weakly, and she shook her head and coughed.

"I didn't want to, but he made me. I never would have—"

Charlie turned away and searched the snow, desperate now, turning his head this way and that.

"Hanna! Hanna!"

Above their heads, the snowfall had faded to just a trickle, and a weak winter sun started to fight its way through the clouds.

Chapter Forty-six

Although it was almost three weeks since what had happened in the mountains, there was still a handful of reporters at the airport. Some of them were camped out, waiting to speak to the parents of the teenagers who had died. Others lurked by the doors, ready to pounce on the daily flood of investigators and forensics experts, to try to glean whatever fragment of new story they could.

A stream of tired faces flowed in a slow procession from the exit ramp of the plane that had just landed, and the remaining reporters moved as a pack in their direction. From the arrivals section of the airport came the flashing of bulbs, and a babble of questions, an attempt to scavenge the last of whatever flesh could still be found on the bare bones of the story.

But tucked away in the corner of the airport's small bar, nobody noticed the young couple who sat at a low table, two steaming cups of coffee clouding the air in front of them. They had been deliberately kept as far away from the press as they could by investigators and Austrian police. The newspaper reports that detailed what had happened in the mountains to the north had been allowed to reveal that there had been survivors, but prohibited from naming or numbering them because of their age, and the severity of what they had been through.

The girl had black hair, hanging loose about her face, the shaven stubble at the sides just starting to grow back in a short, downy fuzz. If you looked closely, you could still see traces of bruising, around one eye, and pale, fading scars from what she had endured, but they would heal, over time. Her head was resting on the shoulder of a handsome but tired-looking teenager with scruffy, dishevelled brown hair. Occasionally, warily, one or both of them would glance up at somebody or other who passed, but they looked and acted no different from any other young couple, students perhaps, their bodies nestled together, their fingers linked.

The paper on the table in front of them was

in German, but a few minutes earlier the girl had translated the headline for her companion – 44 FEARED DEAD IN ALPS INFERNO TRAGEDY.

The girl had relayed the rest of the story quietly, in English, pausing every now and again to register her disbelief. Then she had slumped against the sofa, her head laid comfortably on the boy's shoulder. After a while, her foot slid out on to the nearby table and pushed the newspaper on to the floor.

"I can't believe what's happened. I can't believe they've got away with what they've done. What they've been doing for years."

Hanna felt Charlie grip her fingers more tightly. The bandage had come off her hand days ago, but the stitches that were still in her arm and her chest caught and pulled if she moved too quickly.

"They haven't. They have to live with themselves, live with what they've done. It's over. For good this time. Because of you."

Hanna lifted a finger to her teeth and bit at the rough nail there. "But no one believes us. After all we've said, everything that's up there. No one believes a word of it."

Charlie nodded resignedly and the two of them

leaned back, eyes closed, listening to the jets that came and went beyond the glass outside. It hadn't snowed for days now and Hanna wondered if what they had been through had exhausted what was left of winter, and banished the storms for the rest of the year. Almost unconsciously, she reached up and touched the tiny talisman at her neck, pushing its edges into the skin of her chest.

A plane started to warm up on a runway in the distance, its engines whirring gently, and Hanna looked across at Charlie. "What time is your flight?"

Charlie checked his battered Nixon watch, the glass face more scuffed than ever. "Not for a few hours, not until tonight. Are you bored?"

Hanna shook her head gently. "Never again."

She turned to watch a plane take off, back lights blinking against the grey sky, and she felt a wave of displeasure, like a nasty taste in her mouth.

"And Tara?"

Charlie shrugged. "I've got a feeling that she's gone already. Now that they've decided to stop questioning us every day, I think she's gone home, taken an earlier flight. I've barely seen her, barely spoken to her since they arrived to take us off the mountain."

Hanna sighed. "You know, if not for her, we'd have almost certainly died in there. Her awful screaming. I don't like to admit this, but I think she saved me a second time."

Charlie shook his head in disagreement. "We'd have died a long time before without you. All of us. Anyway, she told me Nico made her go back, she said he wouldn't stay in the hut, and more than anything she didn't want to be alone. If anyone saved us, it was Nico. He was brave in the end, braver than anyone."

Hanna realized that she'd never get a chance to thank Nico for what he'd done, not now, and she felt a flicker of regret. She bent down and retrieved the paper, staring again at the headline there. "What do you think Tara told them?"

Charlie shook his head. "I don't know. It was like, whenever I spoke to any of the investigators, they'd already written off what I was about to say. But if I were in their place, I guess I wouldn't have believed it either. Much easier to believe that a fire swept through half of the village, burning it to the ground, killing everyone while they slept."

Hanna bit at her bottom lip and pushed the paper away. "Somehow, I don't think Tara told them the truth."

Another plane lifted into the sky, and Charlie pushed back his hoodie for a moment and watched it fade into the distance. He turned to Hanna and looked her in the eyes. "Are you sure you won't come?"

Hanna took a weary breath. "I want to. You know I really want to. But I need to spend some time with my parents. They've been through enough already, first Jon, then thinking I was dead, then finding out I wasn't. And if no one else believes me, then at least I can tell *them* the truth."

She absently touched the dolphin around her neck once more. "But I'll be here, when you're finished. How long, do you think?"

"A few days, a week at the most. There's nothing there for me, not now, but I have to say goodbye. My gran, she barely knows me any more, but I have to go back one last time."

Hanna reached up and stroked his face, then leaned forwards and brushed her lips against his.

"I'm here for you. I'll be here waiting. And you're sure? About coming back to the mountains with me? Are you sure it's what you want us to do?"

Hanna smiled, picturing the thick snow melting to reveal the lush grass underneath. "The summer will be beautiful. But the winters can be hard."

Charlie nodded and took her hand. Over his shoulder another plane took off, soaring into the distance, the future ahead.

"There's nowhere I'd rather be."

Epilogue

At thirty-three thousand feet, Tara felt almost alone again for the first time in weeks. Alone, except for the quiet, amiable voice that seemed to now reside somewhere at the back of her head, whispering to her, guiding her through the way ahead like a secret, unseen confidante.

The voice's name was Sabine.

It had been Sabine's idea to not tell the police and interviewers the whole story, and to go along with the tale put forward by the remaining villagers that it had been a fire, sweeping through the deserted streets, taking the lives of most of the students, forcing the few who survived to take refuge in the church above the village. While Tara and the others had gone on Hanna's mad expedition to the caves, a handful of the villagers had crept out, setting fire to the Panoramic Hotel and the surrounding shops, hiding whatever evidence they could, and that had made Tara's story so much easier to swallow.

The thing that used to be Ryan had bitten Tara as she had made her way out into the light. It was only a graze, the teeth of the creature digging into her wrist, before Nico had sacrificed himself to save her. Tara hadn't realized it at the time, but as she scrambled for the light she heard her new friend's voice in her head, guiding her, looking out for her, whispering ways for Tara to get all the things she wanted, things that she had lost in the past but deserved to have again.

The other survivors would have told a different story, Tara suspected, one that more closely resembled what had really happened, but it had been easy for her to subtly discredit the seeds of any story they might have told, Sabine guiding her all the time, getting stronger, more sure, more able to help Tara do what was right. As for the others, Sabine reassured her that Hanna's time would come, soon enough, and she would suffer for the way she had treated them both, for the things she had done.

A passing flight attendant glanced at Tara and her mother, sleeping by the window, and offered Tara a drink from the trolley. Tara thought for a moment, then ordered a glass of champagne. The attendant hesitated, internally assessing the girl's age, but Tara felt Sabine move to the front of her mind, bending the attendant's will to her own. A moment later a fizzing glass of champagne appeared on Tara's table. The woman opened her mouth again to ask for the payment, but another nudge from Sabine banished that idea, too.

It was as if Tara's silent friend could bring people round to her way of thinking, just by a look, by the power of her will. It didn't work on everyone, of course, only the weaker minds. But those it didn't work on were soon disarmed by the tears and hysterics of the traumatized teenage girl, who had been through hell at the top of an isolated mountain.

Tara sat back in her chair, closed her eyes, and heard Sabine start to whisper at her afresh. Outside the plane's tiny window the sun started to set, and Tara felt the voice grow stronger, more assertive, the way it did as night-time came.

For now, the voice whispered, the daylight wasn't a problem. Once Sabine grew stronger, they would need to find a new home, dark, hidden. Somewhere grand and luxurious, somewhere they could be safe, where those that followed them, those that Sabine made join them, could hide from the light, but there was time for that, later.

Things were going to be different now, Sabine promised, and soon Tara was going to get all the things she had ever dreamed of: opulence, jewels, servants who did what she asked, people who would give their lives just to do her bidding.

Before long, Tara would get her revenge on all those that had ridiculed her, mocked her, made her life a misery since her family's money had run out. Soon, people would fall to their knees before her.

Soon.

Acknowledgements

Firstly thanks to Mum and Dad, who hopefully now realize that all those hours spent reading me comics by my bedside lamp and dealing with my horror and fantasy obsessions have finally paid off. Huge thanks to Polly Nolan for finding me in the slush pile and taking a gamble on me, and to the whole of the Stripes team for being an absolute joy to work with, particularly Katie and Charlie, and Mattie, who made editing *Whiteout* a pleasure and saved the world from my awful grammar. I feel privileged to have such a fantastic cover going out into the world with my novel, so huge thanks to Stripes designer Pip Johnson for the stunning artwork. Thanks to Jo Beamish, without whom I'd never have been invited on the trip to Austria that inspired this novel. Thanks also to Giles Potter, Rachel Newman and Aelred Down for letting me steal their teacher names, and to Nicholino 'Lino' Meloscia for letting me borrow his Christian name and his film knowledge. And last but not least, thanks to my wife and best friend, Rachel, for setting off with me on this amazing journey.

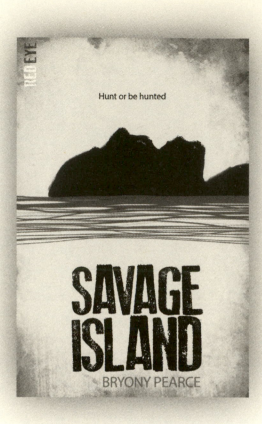

Hunt or be hunted

SAVAGE ISLAND

BRYONY PEARCE

Are you the best?
Are you driven to succeed?

A one million pound prize. Each. That's enough to
get five friends entering a geocaching competition.
But stranded on a remote island off the Scottish coast,
they soon realize this is no ordinary challenge.

The other teams are determined to win too.
Even if it means getting rid of the opposition.
Permanently.

Turn the page for an extract from

BRYONY PEARCE

ISBN: 978-1-84715-827-7

Prologue

"What would you do with a million pounds?"

There was something important behind Lizzie's question; I could tell by the way she kept twisting her short dark hair into knots as she showed us into her room. She was a ball of condensed energy, all excitement.

"You bring us up here for a quiz, Lizzie?" Grady asked as he dumped himself on to a beanbag. His knees almost hit his ears and he grinned. Grady could be a bit odd, but his smile was infectious and Lizzie grinned back.

I leaned my skateboard against the doorway, took a Coke from the six-pack Grady handed me from his bag and passed the rest around. Carmen had already made herself at home and was lying on the bed. She downed half of her can before Lizzie opened hers. My brother, Will, eyed his before taking it, as if wondering what Grady would want from him later if he accepted.

Lizzie was still running her fingers through her pixie-cut. I remembered the row three years earlier when she first wanted the style. Her mum had forbidden it, so Lizzie had hacked off her long plaits with nail scissors.

"I thought we were heading into town?" I said.

"I need to show you something first. Take a seat – it'll take a while to load." She switched on her computer, but remained standing.

As the monitor flickered into life, I looked around her room. The last time I'd been in here, the walls had been pastel pink and we'd spent whole days playing *Legend of Zelda* on her Wii. Now the walls were a light blue-grey, the posters had morphed from Justin Bieber into Nina Simone, and there was a pile of climbing gear in one corner. But it was the same desk; I ran my finger over our initials carved into the right-hand side and smiled. The bed was the same too: plain white ironwork, decorated with home-made paper birds and butterflies wired on to the joins. I sank my feet into the rug, remembering the feel of the wool on my stomach, the controller in my hand and Lizzie beside me.

"What happened to your mum's 'no boys' rule?" Will slid into the chair by the desk. The way his hair was always hanging over his eyes drove me insane, but girls liked it, apparently.

"Seeing as I'll be at uni in a few months, Mum got reasonable." Lizzie didn't take her eyes off the screen.

"I'm *so* glad it's summer. I mean, those exams nearly killed me!" Grady took a sip of his Coke and sighed. "Hey, have you heard about the Coca-Cola conspiracy?" He didn't wait for an answer. "Did you know that Coke is the main cause of the US obesity epidemic? These cans contain, like, over forty milligrams of sodium. That makes you even thirstier, so you drink more. It's why there's so much sugar in it – to hide the salt."

I pointed at the Coke. "So, you don't want it?"

"It's all about making informed choices, Ben. I can have a glass of water after." Grady burped.

Carmen laughed. "You *are* funny, Grady."

Will looked sideways at Carmen, then away.

"OK, ready!" Lizzie turned her monitor so the rest of us could view the display and pointed to a spinning logo. "Check this out."

GOLD

FOUNDATION

Carmen rubbed absentmindedly at the blue kestrel tattooed on the inside of her wrist. "What's the Gold Foundation?"

"It's run by Marcus Gold," Grady jumped in. "The multibillionaire. He owns half of Silicon Valley, runs all those charities, has that airline – Goldstar." He took a deep breath and carried on. "He's rumoured to be part of Yale's Skull and Bones society. He's definitely a Freemason and probably one of the guys behind 9/11, he—"

"The only people behind 9/11 were the terrorists." Lizzie frowned at him.

Grady sighed. "If you'd ever read the information I send you—"

I kicked his beanbag. "We're never going to take anything written by David Icke seriously, Grady. He thought he was the Son of God. Give it up."

"Guys." Lizzie grabbed her mouse and scrolled down the page. "Look!"

IRON TEEN

Are you the best? Are you driven to succeed?
Are you in top physical shape?
Will you be between sixteen and twenty years old on 15th August 2018?
Can you get a team of five together?
Do you want to win £1 million ... each?

Under-eighteens need permission from a parent or guardian to apply.

Grady rolled off his beanbag and moved closer to the screen. "A million pounds *each*!"

"That's what it says." Lizzie nodded excitedly.

Will frowned. "Why is Gold offering so much money?"

"He's a philanthropist," Lizzie said. Grady snorted loudly but she ignored him. "See here, it says he wants to give bright, proactive teens a push in life. The winners get investment advice to help them make the best of their prize money."

"Well … we don't have to *take* the advice," Grady said thoughtfully. "There's a lot I could do with a million pounds."

Carmen began to skim-read the text. "It says we have to fill in a load of assessment forms."

"But what's the competition?" Will put his hands behind his head. "What do we have to do?"

"The teams that pass the assessment stage go into a lottery. Ten teams get chosen and they're flown out to a remote island owned by Gold, where there'll be tests of endurance and intelligence." Lizzie could barely suppress her excitement. "It sounds like orienteering and puzzle-solving along with a bit of geocaching, rock climbing … that kind of thing."

"That sounds great!" I looked at my brother. I hadn't come up with anything to occupy us over the summer. "We'd enter even without the prize money. Right, Will?"

Will shrugged.

"There's nothing in here we can't do." Lizzie bounced on her toes. "We've got Grady's gaming skills for puzzle-solving. Will was the best orienteer when we did Duke of Edinburgh and we all know his brain is a miracle. You can fix practically anything, Ben — and Car, you were brilliant when Noah broke his leg last year. If we pass the assessment and get through the lottery, we could totally win this." Lizzie looked at Carmen. "What do you think?"

"I don't know, *chica*." Carmen avoided her gaze. "I'd have to take time off work. I told the salon I could work full time, starting next week."

"You enjoyed Duke of Edinburgh."

"I liked helping at the animal shelter. But when I agreed to do DofE you promised that we'd have a *fun* summer. This does not sound like fun."

"A million pounds, Car." Will brushed his hair out of his eyes. "It would pay for vet school."

"That was a secret." She glared at him. "A stupid dream."

"You never told me that's what you wanted to do!" Lizzie adjusted her glasses and sat next to her. "You have to come with us. You'd be a fantastic vet!" She smiled. "We can't do it without you."

"Fine." Carmen threw up her hands. "I can always get another floor-sweeping job if I lose this one."

"What about you, Grady?" Lizzie asked.

He grinned. "I'm in if you guys are."

We'd only let Grady join our Duke of Edinburgh squad after Noah's accident left us a man down and his dad put him forward but, despite his oddities, I was glad we had. Grady never went anywhere without his 'bag of tricks' – he took that old Scout motto *Be prepared* to heart. Also, Will seemed to like him, which was a definite plus.

"We're entering, then?" I looked around.

"This is going to be *amazing*, you guys." Lizzie leaped up and clicked on the link to download the entry forms.

My phone blinked and vibrated. "Will, Mum's calling."

"She's calling *you*." Will didn't even look up.

I left my drink and went out to the landing. There was no telling what mood she'd be in. I took a deep breath, let the phone ring for as long as I dared and then accepted the call.

"Where are you?" she snapped.

"Hi, Mum. We're at Lizzie's."

"Will's with you?"

"Where else?"

"Don't take that tone with me." I could picture

her sitting on the chair in the hall, her pale brown fringe hanging over her face. Her hair was just like Will's – mine was ginger, like Dad's. "Are you watching him?"

"He's almost seventeen, Mum."

"You know how delicate he is."

My jaw tightened. "Yes, I'm watching him."

"You have to *be there* for him, Ben."

"Yes, Mum."

"He was the worst affected when your father left."

"I know, Mum."

Her tone changed. "You'd better not be eating anything over there. I've got your dinner on."

"Yes, Mum. I mean, no, we're not eating."

Will and I were only allowed what Mum put on the table. This month we were doing the Atkins diet. I never thought I'd miss carrots and I'd kill for a plate of chips.

"Just like your father! You make promises then you go and do whatever you want." She was working herself up; probably standing now, pacing.

"I'm sorry."

I held the phone away from my ear as she began to yell at me. "… your responsibility … don't you go thinking you're too good..."

I waited until she calmed down, then said, "Everything's fine here, Mum, honestly. We'll be back for dinner."

"Promise?"

"Why don't you make a cup of tea and relax?"

"That's a good idea, Ben." Her voice softened and I sighed. I couldn't figure out if she'd worry more when we left home or less. She was the one who had let Will do his exams a couple of years early and apply to Oxford. She wanted to be able to brag about her genius son.

I took a deep breath. "I'll see you later, OK?"

Will looked up as I walked back in. "The usual?"

I tossed the phone on to the bed. "The usual."

The forms had to be filled in by hand and posted, so Lizzie had printed them out. The others had already started. Carmen hummed tunelessly until Lizzie reached over and switched on her old record player. Nina Simone's deep voice filled the room.

"Are you sure your mum will let you come, Will?" Lizzie asked. Her fingers had gone back to her hair, worrying. I wanted to hold her hand to calm her; I gripped my pen tighter.

"She'll be fine with it," Will said.

I snorted. "She won't be 'fine with it'. But Will should be able to talk her round. It would be easier if we could tell the local paper we were applying – she'd love that. But the prize money should go a long way towards persuading her."

"I don't understand this dumb confidentiality clause – why can't we tell the papers?" Grady frowned. "It seems suspicious to me. If this was all above board, it would be *everywhere*."

"It's on the *Internet*, Grady." Lizzie tapped her pencil impatiently. "It *is* everywhere."

"It's not a bad thing," I said. "The fewer people who know about the competition, the more chance we have of getting through."

"Anyway," Carmen added, "do you really want to be in the papers saying, 'We're entering this competition'? If we lose, everyone will know. If we win, we'll be hounded for the money – it happened to my Uncle Javi."

"You have a millionaire uncle?" I asked.

Carmen let out a laugh. "*Chico!* No! He won a year's supply of ham. All he had, day and night, were calls from people wanting free ham." She rolled off the bed. "I don't know my blood type. I need to call Mami. Can I use someone's phone?"

"Out of credit again?" Lizzie tossed hers over.

Carmen caught Lizzie's phone. "Always." She danced into the hall and down the stairs. "*Buenos días*, Mrs Bellamy. You look lovely today!"

I started my own form while Carmen was out of the room, looking up only when she jumped back on to the bed saying, "I am O negative, by the way."

"That's unusual, isn't it?" Lizzie frowned.

"I am Spanish, remember!" Carmen said, as if that explained it.

"Actually," Grady said, "it means you're descended from the Nephilim … or aliens. Opinion is divided on which it is. I'll send you a link."

Carmen grinned.

"Ben, have you got to part two?" Lizzie asked me. "These questions are nuts – listen to this. *Success is based on survival of the fittest; I don't care about the losers.*"

I turned over my page. "I'm not there yet…"

"What are we meant to answer, though? I mean, what do they want us to say? Look at these." She shoved her form at me.